Christmas At The Manor

Books By
JENNIFER NICE

Christmas At The Manor:
Merry Christmas Eve Eve
That's It In A Nutcracker
All's Fair In Love And Christmas

The Nice Romance Collection
(a series of standalone romances):
Digging the Director
A Scottish Christmas Dream
Let's Skip This Christmas
Yellow Petals At Christmas

Join the
CLUB

Find all of the above books and sign up to the mailing
list for more at
www.writeintothewoods.com/romance

For my mum.
For everything.

Contents

Merry Christmas Eve Eve

JENNIFER NICE

1

'What's the point of fruit cake?' asked Eve, leaning against the wall in the pristine professional kitchen of the Flour Power Bakery.

'One of your five a day,' said Beth. 'Technically, it's healthy.'

'Well,' said Eve. 'If you're going to throw logic at me then this is an argument I can't win.'

Beth grinned as she finished rolling out the white icing for the last Christmas cake.

'Make yourself useful,' she said. 'Start mixing some icing for the cupcakes. They'll be ready soon.' She caught sight of Eve's expression and pointed a finger at her friend. 'No! No eating anything.'

Eve laughed and went to fetch the ingredients. She followed Beth's instructions, putting the icing sugar and butter into the mixer and then they both jumped back as Eve turned the mixer on. A cloud of icing sugar erupted from the bowl and Eve danced and twirled in the cloud.

'Now it's Christmas!'

Beth laughed. Her hair was long and dark, matching her long eyelashes over her chocolate brown eyes. As she spent so much time in her professional kitchen, she nearly always had her hair tied tightly back in a low ponytail or, as today, hidden beneath a flour coated baseball cap.

'Really? Now it's Christmas? I would have thought you'd save that for the chocolate yule log waiting for you in the fridge.'

Eve stopped twirling and stared at her friend.

'Please don't be joking.'

'Would I joke about such a thing? Just promise me you won't eat it all at once. Savour it.'

'Of course. I always savour everything you make.'

'That's true. It does take you ages to eat even the wedding cake tasters I make.'

'Well, that's your own fault. They melt in the mouth.' Eve opened one of the large fridges that dominated the back wall and stared open-mouthed at the five chocolate yule logs waiting in there. 'Well, I don't know what to say. You didn't have to make me five.'

'Oh, good. I can spare four for the shop, then?' Beth teased.

Eve shrugged.

'I suppose so. Would hate for you to go out of business.'

Grinning, Beth beckoned for Eve to return to the mixer.

'Pay attention to what you're doing.'

'Sorry, Chef.' Eve returned to watch the icing turn over and over. The twinkling sound of Carol of the Bells began playing and Eve apologised, taking out her phone. She frowned at the name on the screen.

'Who is it?' asked Beth.

'No idea.' Eve answered the phone, holding it up to her ear. 'Hello?'

'Hello, is this a Miss Dutton?'

'Speaking.'

'My name's Jeff Hargreaves, Stanley Hargreaves is – was – my father.'

Eve held her breath and then, blinking as her eyes grew hot, she murmured, 'Was?'

The man on the end of the phone sighed.

'My father passed away two nights ago.'

Eve's knees weakened and she groped for something to sit on. Beth, watching her, grabbed a chair from the corner of the room and Eve plonked onto it.

'How?' she murmured.

'His heart just stopped.' Jeff's voice had grown weak and soft but Eve's mind was racing too fast to acknowledge it.

'I'm sorry,' was all she could manage. 'I saw him four days ago,' she added. 'He was his usual self.'

'I understand he had a couple of events booked with you?' Jeff continued.

'Erm. Yeah. A ghost tour and a murder mystery.

One for Christmas and one for New Year.' Eve found the words on autopilot, the organised part of her brain clicking into action.

'I'm afraid we'll need to cancel.'

Eve blinked.

'Oh... I... Right.' She searched hard for the right words as her mind span. Cancelling would cost her money, not just in lost expenses but in lost income. What about the people who had bought tickets? The people who were looking forward to the events? But, on the other hand, Stanley Hargreaves had passed away. She could hardly hold the events without him and so soon after his death, especially in his own home. 'No. Of course. Okay.' A single tear dropped down her cheek as her vision blurred.

Beth had turned the mixer off and was watching her friend, her fingers playing at her apron.

'Thank you for understanding,' said Jeff.

'It's just that,' Eve added quickly. 'Everything's booked. The actors are booked. I'll still need to pay them. And the ghost tour is tomorrow evening. It's a tradition. Stan, erm, Mr Hargreaves always insisted.'

'Okay. But... Look, we're going through his estate now. Everything's in upheaval. There's no time for any events. And really? A ghost tour and a murder mystery?'

'Yeah, no, I understand, but your father loved those events. It's why he let me use the house for free.' Eve snapped her mouth shut as Beth's eyes widened.

'Free?' came Jeff's voice.

Eve scrunched her eyes shut. She shouldn't have said that.

'Well, it was his house,' she answered feebly.

'Right.'

There was an awkward silence.

'So, you'll cancel the events,' said Jeff eventually.

Eve looked up at Beth imploringly, as if her friend had any idea as to what was going on.

'But it's Christmas,' she said softly.

'Yes, Miss Dutton. And I'm facing my first Christmas without my father.' Jeff's voice broke a little at that and Eve silently scolded herself. 'I'm afraid the events must be cancelled. Thank you.' He hung up without waiting for her reply.

Slowly, Eve lowered her phone and stared up at Beth.

'What's happened?' her friend asked.

Eve couldn't hold back any longer. She promptly burst into tears and shook her head apologetically, excusing herself with a hand gesture and disappearing into the little staff toilet at the back of Beth's bakery.

When she returned, her eyes still red but the sobs quietened, she sat back in the chair and put her head in her hands.

'Stan died two nights ago,' she said quietly.

'Oh, love.' Beth was by her side in a second, wrapping her arms around Eve. 'I'm so sorry.'

Eve hugged her back.

'That was his son on the phone. He says the Christmas events are cancelled.'

Beth frowned and went to argue but then softened.

'Well, I guess it's probably poor taste to run a ghost tour and murder mystery in Stan's house days after he's died.'

Eve nodded.

'Yeah.'

'And the man has just lost his dad.'

'Yeah.' Eve sniffed.

Beth squeezed her.

'It'll be okay. It's just one small business set back. You wouldn't feel able to run those events without Stan, anyway, would you?'

Eve began to shake and Beth pulled away.

'Hang on.' She made her way over to the fridge. 'You need something for the shock.'

'You're not bringing me eggnog, are you?' Eve said, smiling despite herself.

Beth grinned.

'I was wondering if we had any brandy left. Ah, here we go.' She pulled out a small bottle from beside the fridge and opened it, pouring a splash into a measuring cup and handing it to Eve. 'It'll make you feel better,' she urged.

Eve sipped at the brandy and pulled a face, then she downed the lot in one go. Her throat and stomach burned, the heat rushing through her and within seconds, she did feel better.

'Poor Stan,' she murmured.

'How did it happen?' Beth asked, leaning against the fridge and crossing her arms.

'He said his heart just gave out.'

'Well, he was old.'

'Ninety-two.'

'Blimey. And he had a really good life.'

Eve smiled.

'Yeah. He was full of life. He always had a story to tell and he always wanted to be moving, even when he couldn't move far himself. That's why he loved the events, that's why he let me hold them there for free. Oh, Beth.' Eve looked up at her friend. 'What am I going to do? It's not just these two events, is it. I've lost my venue, haven't I. No more ghost tours or murder mysteries at the Manor. Ever. I haven't just lost Stan. What if I lose my business?' Fresh, hot tears were building in Eve's eyes.

'Nope. You always said to me that when life throws you a blockade, you adapt and build around it. Remember?' said Beth. 'Remember when that wedding cake shop opened across the road? Remember what you told me to do?'

'I told you to specialise and go big.'

'You did. And what did I do?'

'You went big and managed to get double spread features in a load of big wedding magazines.'

'And what happened?'

'You survived.' Eve sighed.

'And?'

Eve looked up at Beth, blinking back the tears. 'And?' she asked.

'And my revenue went through the roof. I bought my flat that year, remember?'

Eve looked down at her lap.

'Oh, yeah.'

'So, Stan passing away has put a blockade in your business. What are you going to do once you've grieved for your friend?'

Eve sighed and sat back, looking at the empty measuring cup in her hand.

'Win the lottery and buy the Manor house off his family?'

Beth hesitated.

'I mean, I suppose I was thinking of something that didn't involve winning the lottery.'

'It would be nice, though, wouldn't it. If the house was mine.'

'Well, yeah... You know,' said Beth thoughtfully. 'Stan loved you. Maybe he's left you something. Some money or something. Heaven knows the man was loaded. Something that you could invest into the business to help you through this.'

Eve frowned. As helpful as that would be, she didn't like the idea of relying on him having left her money. He wasn't a relative, he wasn't part of the business, he'd just been a dear friend who loved socialising and chatting and watching people have fun.

'Maybe. But I doubt it,' she said carefully.

'Well, I guess you can't rely on it,' Beth mused.

Eve sighed and ran her hand over her damp face.

'I'm going to have to let all of those people down. Both events had sold out.' She groaned and held out the measuring cup as Beth offered her more brandy. She sipped at it this time and wiggled her toes in her boots. 'If they put the house on the market, maybe I could look into buying it. It'd be a great investment. I could hold all sort of events there and you could open a little café there. Just think.'

Beth didn't reply and when Eve looked up at her, her friend was giving her a look.

'Yeah. I know. I could never afford it.' Then Eve's eyes brightened. 'We could afford it together? What if we buy it together?'

'You don't even know if they'll sell it,' said Beth. 'Why would they? Stan told you it's been in the family for generations, didn't he? How many kids does he have?'

'Three or four.'

'Right, so they won't sell it. They might argue over it. He's probably left it to them.'

'Maybe whoever gets it would be open to using it as an event space.'

'Eve.' Beth crouched down in front of her friend and waited until she had Eve's full attention. 'Stop thinking. Let it go. At least until after Christmas.

They just lost their dad. And you just lost a good friend. Okay? Go and cancel the events, take the hit, and if you like and you need the money, I can swing you a couple of shifts here. We'll be rushed off our feet, so any extra help would be great. If nothing else, it'll take your mind off it. Then, in the New Year, we can start looking for a new venue. A better venue. How about that?'

Eve nodded. Beth was right. Of course, she was right, and with that admission, Eve's chest began to ache. New tears built in her eyes but she blinked them back and sniffed.

'Right. No, you're right. Okay. I'll go cancel on everyone. You're right.' Eve stood and handed Beth the measuring cup just as Carol of the Bells began playing again. Numb, Eve took out her phone and recognised the number that had rung before. 'It's Stan's son again.'

'Answer it. Maybe he's changed his mind,' said Beth.

2

'Hello?' Eve answered her phone.

'Hi. It's Jeff Hargreaves again. Sorry. We just found some strange stuff in a cupboard. I'm guessing it's something to do with the events you hold here?'

Eve clenched her eyes shut, picturing exactly what he was talking about.

'Yeah. Yes, those are the event props.' Eve pinched the space between her eyes.

'Interesting,' said Jeff. 'When can you come and get them?'

Something in Eve's chest twisted.

'Oh. It's just... Maybe we could talk about the events? I mean, obviously I'll cancel the two coming up, but after that...' Eve drifted off, hoping Jeff would fill in the gaps.

'No. I'm afraid you won't be able to hold any more of these things here. Sorry,' he added as an afterthought, which was something.

Eve swallowed hard to stop herself from crying

again.

'Well, maybe it's something we could discuss after Christmas?' she attempted.

'Look. I know my dad loved these things, he loved all of those types of things. But we just can't feasibly do it anymore. I've got enough going on right now, all right? I don't need someone begging me to hold a stupid murder mystery in my family's home at Christmas when my dad's just...' Jeff sighed into the phone and Eve bit her lip, the tears filling her eyes.

She sniffed loudly and nodded as she gulped down a sob.

'Right. No. Of course.' There was a quiver in her voice that she just couldn't hide. 'Just... Stan really did love these things,' she murmured pitifully.

'Dad loved lots of silly things,' said Jeff. 'When can you come and collect it all?'

The second remark about her business being anything but serious was the one that found its way inside Eve. It wiggled and buried itself, and with another sniff, some anger was released.

'Well, bah humbug to you too. I'll come now, shall I? Get this all over with so you can be rid of me.' Eve hung up without letting Jeff respond and then instantly regretted it. She closed her eyes and took a deep breath. The poor man had just lost his father and she was screaming 'bah humbug' at him. What did that make her?

She blinked back another wave of tears. She

didn't deserve them, she didn't deserve to feel sorry for herself.

Eve wandered back into the kitchen where Beth was carefully trimming the icing from the cake. She stopped as Eve appeared and plonked herself back onto the chair.

'Got any more alcohol?'

'Why? What did he say? What happened?'

'I'm an idiot, Beth,' Eve murmured. 'I called him a bah humbug.'

Beth smothered a smirk.

'Oh, Eve.'

'He's found the props Stan let me stash at the house. I have to go pick them up.'

'When? Do you want me to come with you?'

'No. That's okay. It won't take long and I'll have more room in the car if it's just me. I can fill up the passenger seat. And anyway, you've got a thriving business to run.'

Beth sighed.

'So have you,' she said, wrapping her arms around Eve and giving her a tight hug. 'But let yourself feel first, okay? Go get your stuff, say good-bye to the house, grieve, eat Christmas food and then we'll sit down and figure out your next steps. Together. All right?'

Eve nodded, still fighting the tears as she hung onto Beth's arms. She mentally shook herself and fetched her coat and bag.

'All right. Here we go. Now or never. Or later, I

guess. But now it is. I'll call you later?'

'Definitely,' said Beth, returning to her cake. 'Be careful driving.'

Eve left the bakery, weaving around the tables of couples, friends and families all chatting and sliding their forks through soft cakes, sipping at coffees. She passed the steamed up windows, delicately decorated with festive stickers, and out onto the cold December high street. The door shut behind her and the sound of happy chatter and scent of coffee left her. Eve paused for a moment on the pavement while she wrapped her scarf around her chin and lips. There was a heavy chill in the air that forced her eyes to the sky and the ominous grey clouds that had to be heavy with snow.

Eve hadn't checked the weather recently and it was a shock to see those clouds. Perhaps it was no bad thing that she would have to cancel the events once she was home. The tears sprang forth then. Stan would have loved the snow. She would have driven up the long driveway to the manor house and he would have been waiting, standing on the porch, in a bobble hat and tightly wrapped scarf but with his coat undone, excited to see the first flakes fall. Janine, his housekeeper of thirty years, would have appeared behind him, chastising him for going outside without his coat done up properly, and Stan would have challenged her, a big grin on his face, that he was indeed still technically inside the house, being under the shelter of the porch.

Eve smiled.

She would miss that big grin of his and the way it lit up his eyes, grown light with age but still twinkling whenever he was excited or happy. Eve tried to remember other things about him, bringing to mind anything vivid, as she walked to her car and dug around in her bag for her keys.

Quite a few things made his eyes twinkle. Whenever she'd brought cakes from Beth's shop for him to taste, when the leaves started to change in autumn, at the first sign of the daffodils poking through the soil in spring, at the request of a story from his youth, whenever he talked about his children and wife. Christmas, however, excited Stan more than anything else.

Eve frowned as she started the ignition, trying to remember their conversations about Stan's family. He'd lost his wife fifteen years earlier after a long illness. His voice had broken every time he mentioned her, and each time it caught at Eve's heart, as the memory did now.

Did he have three children or four? There were two boys, she remembered that much. The eldest and the youngest were his sons, but were there one or two daughters in the middle? Eve didn't know their names or which son Jeff was. Stan had spoken of all of them highly, with great pride and love, so it had always been quite hard to tell them apart. The eldest was divorced and the youngest had never married, she remembered that much. Stan wasn't a fan of his daughter's husband. Last time they'd spoken of it, he'd been gossiping that something wasn't right in the relationship and that perhaps it was nearing the end. He'd been hoping for a divorce by Christmas. Eve hadn't given an opinion on the topic, not knowing the people involved, but it had seemed a little mean of Stan to want something like that for his daughter. And what of the other daughter? Was she happily married or did she not exist? Eve laughed despite herself, as if that's all there was in life. To be happily married or to not exist. Stan had certainly not believed that. He'd talked for hours about how proud he was of his children's careers and families. As long as they were happy, he'd always say, then he was happy.

Eve drove through the town, reaching the edge and passing into the countryside. There was something peaceful about having open fields on either side, even as the road narrowed. She knew these roads so well, having held events at Stan's house for a few years. She'd been the one to approach him. Within weeks of starting her events business, she'd been scouting venues and had driven past the Manor. It was stunning and Gothic-looking, perfect for a murder mystery. She'd immediately driven home to research the property and discovered a ghost story set in the grounds. If it hadn't been for that, she probably would never have thought about holding ghost tours. The next day, before she lost her nerve, she'd driven back to the Manor, up the imposing driveway and knocked on the door. Janine had answered and, knowing her employer well, had disappeared into the house to mention it to Stan. Eve had expected to be told he'd call her back, only to never hear from him, so she'd been shocked in the best of ways when Stan had appeared at the door and invited her in for a tour. From the beginning, he'd been warm, friendly and thrilled to hear all of her ideas. She'd asked him for a venue hire quote then but he wouldn't hear of it. Instead, he'd offered her a deal. She could hold the events in the house for free, as long as nothing was broken or damaged of course, and in return, he would be able to attend and take part in every single event.

Eve couldn't have agreed any faster.

Stan had always been fun-loving. He just wanted his last years to be filled with laughter and joy, and that had become his mission. Sure, he'd slowed down since Eve had first met him, and sometimes he coughed after laughing. He'd had to start sitting more often and watching the events from afar rather than being directly involved. That was why she'd started running more murder mysteries, held in the grand sitting room with a roaring fire. It was also why Stan had started placing gadgets around the house whenever there was a ghost tour, so that wherever he was, unable to join in, he would be able to hear their gasps and yelps of fear and surprise. Eve and Janine had both worked hard to convince him to keep those frights to a minimum, and only let him do exactly what he wanted on the Halloween tours.

Christmas is about gentle spirits, Eve had often told him when it came time for the Christmas ghost tour. Think the Ghosts of Christmas Past, Present and Future rather than the Woman in Black.

Stan had reluctantly agreed and then earlier that year had hired a local girl on her black horse to ride through the Manor's grounds while wearing a long black cloak. It had led to screaming and one woman feeling faint, especially when the sound of a rocking chair came through the ceiling from the attic above. Eve had almost worried until every single customer on the tour claimed they would be returning the following year.

Well, that wouldn't be happening now.

Eve wondered then if she'd ever hold another ghost tour. They'd been Stan's favourite event and she'd only had the idea because of his house. Somehow, it didn't seem quite right to run them without him. They wouldn't be as good, for one thing, without his ideas.

Eve turned into the driveway of the Manor and drove towards the large house with its three floors and Gothic edges. The tall trees on either side of the driveway were bare, save for the twinkling lights wrapped around each trunk, giving an excellent view of the gardens in dull greens and browns, sleeping through the winter. Eve sighed. What would happen to the gardens now that Stan wasn't there to hand them over to the two retired gentlemen from the town who busied themselves there all summer? The gardens had been their project once they'd left their office jobs and Stan had pretty much let them do whatever they wanted. Small hedges and beautifully pruned shrubs had popped up along with glorious flower beds of bright colours, pathways of short lush grass leading around them, to a small orchard of apple and pear trees. That orchard had come in handy for the ghost tours, where the group would stop for one of Beth's toffee apples or a freshly baked mince pie.

Something in Eve gave way as she parked up outside the house, next to a large Land Rover and a smaller, sleek BMW.

3

Eve tapped the top of her steering wheel. She didn't want to get out of the car. To get out and knock on the door would be to confirm that Stan wouldn't be answering. Instead, she stayed in her car a moment longer, looking out over the gardens and up at the house, trying hard to memorise every tiny detail about them. The clouds were becoming heavier, if that was possible, and a chill ran through Eve as the car cooled down. With another deep sigh, she got out, tightened her scarf and coat around her and headed for the porch. Stan always decorated, or rather directed Janine how to decorate, the house at the beginning of December, and nothing had changed about the decorations since Eve's last visit to the house four days ago. There was a sprig of mistletoe hanging over the door under the porch. Every Christmas, Stan planted a crafty kiss on every woman's cheek who happened to pass through the front door. There was also greenery and holly around the wooden beams, probably taken from the gardens at the back. Eve choked back a sob as she stepped onto the doorstep and rang the bell. The sound echoed through the house and she listened with her eyes closed, her chest tightening as she waited for someone who wasn't Stan to open the door.

The sound of the latch being lifted and the lock being turned made her slowly open her eyes and look up at the man standing in the doorway. His hair was a soft light brown and grown a little too long in her opinion. It was close to flopping in his eyes and meant that he had to keep sweeping his hand through it to push it back. His eyes were blue and hard, staring down at her as he frowned, etching lines into his forehead and the corner of his eyes. It was an expression that was so far away from Stan's beaming grin that Eve couldn't stop the tears falling down her cheeks.

'I'm here to collect my props,' she managed to say, her voice cracking. The man didn't move at first and when he did, it was to lean forward and look up at the sky. Confused, Eve followed his gaze and then looked back to him.

'Is it snowing?' he asked.

'Not yet,' she told him. 'Looks like it will.'

'Is that fake snow?'

'What?'

'In your hair.' He gestured at her face and Eve's eyes widened.

'Oh.' She pulled a hand through her hair and

then, as the man looked on disgusted, she tasted what was on her fingers. 'It's icing sugar,' she said, a smile twitching at her lips. Stan would have laughed, *Been dancing in the kitchen again, have we?*

This man didn't ask that, but the frown turned into something softer and more curious.

'My friend owns a bakery,' she explained. 'I was helping to make icing when...' Her smile fell. 'When I got the call about...'

The man's expression also fell.

'You're Eve Dutton? Jeff Hargreaves.' He held out a hand which Eve found strange, although she took it without thinking. They shook and then Jeff seemed to realise what he'd done. He took his warm hand back a little too quickly and actually gave his head a little shake. She watched him, her hand still warm from his.

'Come in,' he told her, moving aside.

Eve took a step forward and then stopped before taking a few steps back.

'What are you doing?'

'Hang on,' she said, flipping her hair over her head and giving it a ruffle with her hands. It wasn't as long as Beth's but hung just below her shoulders and when Eve was feeling generous she would call it a caramel brown. It still did a good flick, the icing sugar dropping in front of her in a small cloud. When she flicked her hair back, she smoothed it down and caught Jeff with a surprised look on his face. 'Don't want to leave icing sugar in the house,' she told him before doing a double take at his eyes. Now that they'd softened, even a little, there was something about them. Something familiar. Eve smiled as Jeff led her into the house. They may have been brighter with youth, but Jeff had his father's eyes.

Eve stopped in the middle of the large square hallway. In the corner was the impressive staircase leading around the wall and up to the first floor with its decadent red carpet and sparkling gold trim. The polished oak panelling, which led to a sitting room on the right, an office space on the left and the kitchen straight ahead, was glistening in the twinkling fairy lights that adorned the tall Christmas tree. The tree was where it always was, although this one was taller than last year's. Positioned in the corner of the staircase so that you could stand on the stairs to decorate it, the tree was festooned with glass baubles, toy trinkets and sparkling trails of gold. On the top, an angel was awkwardly perched looking like she'd much rather be where there wasn't the top of a tree poking up her skirt.

Eve stared up at the angel, her eyes aching as she remembered watching Stan standing on the stairs, carefully placing the angel on top of the tree while apologising to it. She swallowed a sob down, making her chest ache.

'Dad always liked to decorate early. It's been this

way since the first of December. He sent me a photo of the tree once it was up,' came Jeff's voice from behind her. He was staring up at the tree too, although Eve didn't dare look at him properly. She tried to wipe her eyes on her sleeve without him noticing but failed.

'I always decorate on the first too,' she said, trying to keep her voice level. 'I was always jealous of how much space Stan has – had. I always dream-ed of having a tree this big.'

From the corner of her eye, she could see Jeff looking at her.

'Yes. Well. Your stuff is over here. I found it in a cupboard.'

'I'm surprised you're going through everything so soon,' said Eve, following Jeff further into the hallway. Everything in this house seemed large, even the cupboards and what Stan referred to as "cosy nooks".

'Oh, it's all the legal stuff. Dad left a will but there's inheritance tax and a load of other stuff I don't really understand. I tend to leave that to my sister. She's a solicitor. It's her firm dealing with it all.'

Eve nodded.

'I wouldn't understand all that stuff either,' she told him. He gave her a small smile and opened the cupboard door.

'To be honest, I thought this was all Dad's until I saw your name on some of it.'

'Yeah. Stan bought some of his own so we needed to know what belonged to who.' Eve reached out and pulled on the flap of a cardboard box full of costumes. Eve's name was scrawled on the side. She frowned. That was new. She ran her fingers over her name.

'I didn't know he'd done this. This wasn't here before.' She looked up at Jeff. 'Did he know he was...' she drifted off, unable to finish the sentence. Jeff's features softened further and he became more familiar. There was something about his lips and the twitch of his mouth. She'd seen it before.

'He'd been ill for a while. You didn't know?'

Eve's stomach twisted with a sickening lurch.

'No. Why wouldn't he tell me,' she murmured. 'What was wrong?'

'His heart,' said Jeff. 'He had a heart attack when he was in his eighties. I always thought he did really well after that, considering. We had to force him to slow down, but now I realise that he didn't slow down as much as I would have liked.' He turned to look over the contents of the cupboard. Eve followed his gaze.

'But it made him happy,' she said softly.

Jeff's eyes returned to her and she slowly turned to meet them.

'He mentioned you, you know.'

Eve blinked. She hadn't been expecting that.

'Really? What did he say?'

'Don't worry, it was all good things. He didn't

mention the events, just said a nice young woman called Eve often dropped by with treats. I worried for a moment until he reassured me that he meant cakes.'

Eve almost laughed.

'From your friend's bakery, I assume?' Jeff continued.

'She makes the best,' Eve told him.

'I had to tell him off. Cake isn't – wasn't good for his heart.'

'He never told me about the heart attack. Otherwise I would have been more careful,' Eve assured him, although she questioned the statement as soon as it left her mouth. If she gave it proper thought and allowed for Stan's inevitable argument, she still would have brought the cakes round. He was over ninety and he'd earned them. That's what he would have said and she'd have been inclined to agree.

'When was the last time you saw him?' asked Jeff.

Eve sighed, pulling out a wide-brimmed hat with a large feather from the cupboard and putting it on without thinking. Jeff smiled at her although it came with confusion.

'Only four days ago, although it seems like a long time now. We met to go over arrangements for the Christmas events. The last event before these was on Halloween. We always did a ghost tour and Stan ended up turning it into a haunted house event that ended in the orchard.' Eve smiled at the memories. 'Stan made it more fun than I ever could have. And my friend provided toffee apples and Stan's friends arranged apple bobbing. It wouldn't have been much without them. I just had the basic idea and hired the medium.'

'Medium?'

'To do the tour. She takes everyone round the house seeing if she can sense ghosts.'

Jeff raised an eyebrow.

'You don't really believe in ghosts, do you?'

'What does that matter?' Eve asked, swapping her hat for another, this time a small Victorian bowler hat.

'I mean, you don't believe she can sense ghosts?'

'I don't know. Did you know that it's illegal to claim that she can? Sort of. She fully believes that she can sense and talk to ghosts but legally she has to call herself an actor and say it's all for entertainment purposes. Do you know why?'

'Why?' asked Jeff, glancing up at the bowler hat on Eve's head.

'Because otherwise she's breaking a law that originated as the Witchcraft Act. Isn't that great? Basically, if she claims it's all real then she's a witch in the eyes of the law. In a roundabout sort of way.'

Jeff held her gaze for a little too long. Eve wilted a little. His eyes were too bright and too blue and she was pretty sure that she just saw a twinkle. She looked away quickly, taking off the bowler hat and replacing it with a cowboy hat.

'I always liked that fact,' she added and stopped rifling through the cupboard to stare into empty space. 'Yeah. Four days ago. Not even a week. I brought mince pies and we ate them around the fire in the sitting room while we made plans.'

Jeff stood silently beside her, perhaps lost in his own memories and regrets.

'He liked you,' he murmured. 'A lot. You brought a lot of fun into his life and I guess that had more to do with these events than the cakes. So, thank you.'

Eve turned to look Jeff in the eye.

'I owe your father so much,' she said gently, aware of a new wave of tears building. 'So, emptying the cupboard,' she added as Jeff's eyes softened again. She turned back to the boxes and started to pull bits and pieces out.

'Yes. I'll help. Is it all going in your car? Will it fit?'

'Should do,' said Eve, filling her arms with a bag of ghostly decorations and placing the bowler hat on top of the cowboy hat already on her head. 'Fill up the car and then when I get it all home, I need to cancel the events.'

'You haven't done that yet?'

'I haven't exactly had time to sit down with a list of names yet.'

'But isn't it tomorrow?'

Eve stopped and turned back to Jeff, precariously balancing the hats above her.

'Yes.'

'So, shouldn't you have cancelled it immediately?'

'You mean immediately after you told me Stan had passed away while I was sobbing my eyes out in my friend's kitchen or immediately after you told me to come and empty the cupboard?'

Jeff hesitated.

'Won't they be angry at the short notice?'

Eve shrugged and then dropped the bag of decorations as she reached out to stop the bowler hat falling off.

'I'm sure they'll understand when I tell them about Stan. They can't really argue that, can they.'

'No. I guess not. And you'll have to refund them all.'

'Of course,' said Eve, picking up the bag of decorations while trying to keep her head straight and the hats balanced.

'So, you'll be out of pocket.'

'I did mention that, didn't I?'

Jeff watched Eve as she slowly turned back towards the front door.

'What if we held the ghost tour?' he said.

Eve stopped and gently turned back.

'Excuse me?' she said, stepping towards him, wondering if she'd heard right or if the hats on her head had somehow muffled the words.

'What's going on here?' came a deep voice. Jeff and Eve both turned to the man who had spoken and both the bowler hat and cowboy hat fell off Eve's head, bouncing on the parquet flooring.

4

The man watched the bowler hat roll for a moment before it settled on the polished floor, then he looked up at Eve. She gave him a quick smile and then tried to dive for the door.

'This is Eve Dutton,' said Jeff. 'She's the one who runs the events Dad used to have here. She's just here to collect her stuff. This is Glen, my brother,' Jeff told Eve.

Eve, struggling with the bag of decorations in her arms, gave Glen another smile and a nod. He looked her up and down, his gaze landing on the bag.

'What stuff? She was keeping stuff here?'

'She's in the room,' Eve muttered before trying to open the front door without any free hands. She sighed and looked back to Jeff for help.

'Props. For the events,' said Jeff, picking up the hats.

'What sort of events need props?'

'A murder mystery,' Eve told Glen. He raised an eyebrow at her. 'Everyone's encouraged to take on the role of a character. Stan would usually sit in the corner and watch so we created a character for him.'

'Let me guess, he'd be the elderly, wealthy man being used for his house and not getting paid?'

Eve reeled, rocking back on her heels and blinking at the force of Glen's anger. She opened her mouth to speak but the words wouldn't come. Thankfully, Jeff managed to find the right thing to say.

'Oh, come on, Glen. Dad would have loved it. You know that.' Jeff reached around Eve and opened the door for her. Thanking him quietly, she walked through and dumped the bag of decorations by her car. Glen and Jeff stayed inside the house so she returned, keeping her head down, meaning to retrieve the hats from Jeff.

To her surprise, he had put the bowler hat on despite being seemingly in a deep conversation, or perhaps argument, with his brother. Eve stopped. There was something almost handsome about Jeff Hargreaves in a bowler hat, although handsome wasn't something that Eve generally liked. She preferred quirky and fun, in both her friends and the men she let into her life. Stan had been quirky and fun. The smile faded from her face at the memory of his grin as he'd put on the flat cap that was currently still in the box in the cupboard. He'd take the cap and an elegant silver-topped walking cane and sit in the corner, leaning forward, taking part as much as he could even as the warm fire attempted to lull anyone who'd had more than one drink to sleep.

'You need to grow up,' Glen was saying.

'And you need to relax,' Jeff retorted. He bit his lip and sighed as Glen's eyes became noticeably watery. 'I'm sorry. I didn't mean that.'

Glen shook his head and rubbed at his eyes. Something inside Eve shifted.

'How can you wear that thing right now?' Glen murmured, glancing at the bowler hat.

Slowly, Jeff took it off and handed it to Eve. She muttered an apology, taking the hat and darting around the men, back to the cupboard.

'Here you both are,' came a woman's voice. When Eve walked back through carrying the box of hats, there was a woman with hair the same colour as Jeff's and eyes the same as Glen's. She stopped when she saw Eve and Jeff once again explained what was going on as Eve dodged around them and outside to her car.

When she re-entered the house, she stopped and sighed, preparing herself.

'I'm so sorry, about your father. Stan was an amazing man,' she told them. 'I didn't know him for that long, really, but some of my favourite memories from the last few years are of being in this house, and your father had some incredible ideas.'

'That was Dad,' the woman murmured, glancing

at Jeff.

'This is my sister, Wendy.'

Eve gave Wendy a smile which Wendy did her best to return. She was a tall woman with long flowing hair and there was something equally intimidating and friendly about her. Eve wasn't sure whether to relax around her or be cautious. She was just about to skirt around the group to return to the cupboard and avoid having to decide how to act when Wendy spoke.

'Dad did like his fun.' She looked appraisingly at Eve. 'And you just ran events here?'

Eve may not have known how to take Wendy, but she knew she didn't like that tone. She narrowed her eyes at Wendy and reminded herself that the woman had just lost her father.

'Stan was always kind and respectful to me, and generous. We had a business arrangement, that I could use his house as a venue but only if he could take part in each event. For which I am truly grateful, because his ideas made the events better. I know he only gave me the ideas so he could have more fun.'

Wendy pursed her lips and then shrugged, turning to her brothers.

'Won't you be lonely here, Jeff? It's a very large house for one man. I was always telling Dad that. Maybe you should stay in your London flat.'

Realising she'd been dismissed, Eve wandered slowly around the siblings and back to the cupboard, pricking her ears as she went.

'If you're about to suggest we sell this place, you can forget it,' came Glen's voice as Eve reached the cupboard. She stopped and stared at the remaining few boxes, not moving. 'It's staying in the family. That's what Dad wanted and it'll be in his will.'

'Of course I'm not suggesting we sell it,' Wendy snapped. 'I'm saying that Jeff can't fill it.'

'Oh, thanks. You don't see me having children and dogs to fill it?'

'You don't even have a girlfriend, so when are you planning on having these children?'

There was a snort which Eve assumed was Jeff.

'Let me guess, you want the house?'

'At least I have children to fill it with voices,' said Wendy.

'You already have your family home.' That was Glen. 'This house was always going to be Jeff's. That's what Dad always said.'

'You know, technically, the eldest should get it,' said Wendy.

'Yeah, well, the eldest is saying that it's Jeff's. End of conversation.' There was a clap, which must have been Glen punctuating the end of his sentence. 'And as I said, it'll be in Dad's will, so there's no argument to have.'

'Fine. But you're not doing what Dad did and running a business from this place. This is our family home,' said Wendy.

'Of course not.' Although Jeff's voice had lost

some of its power. Eve held her breath, willing him to say more. She exhaled in a puff when he appeared beside her, giving her a strange look, and then testing the weight of the nearest box.

'Everything okay?' he asked.

Eve nodded.

'You were saying,' she murmured. 'About holding the last ghost tour?'

Jeff looked into her eyes and Eve's stomach twisted pleasurably. She looked away before she could fully register it, checking inside one of the boxes that she already knew contained costumes. There was something increasingly attractive about Jeff. It was probably the knowledge that he'd be getting the house. She was being vain and shallow. Eve steadied herself. It was just a hint of envy, morphing into an attraction for the wealthy, single man beside her who had what she wanted. That was all. It didn't mean anything.

'Yeah. Dad would have liked that, wouldn't he.'

Eve glanced sideways at Jeff. Was he talking to her or himself?

'They're reading his will once all the red tape is dealt with,' he continued.

'Hmm? Oh. Yes,' said Eve, frowning. How was she supposed to respond to that? 'Red tape?' she asked, fumbling for words.

'Yeah. Legal stuff. I don't know. That's Wendy's thing.'

'Right.'

Jeff smiled to himself.

'Do you know why she's called Wendy?'

Eve straightened and gave this some thought. Finally, she turned to Jeff, grinning.

'Because of Peter Pan? Stan always seemed so young at heart.'

'He used to read us Peter Pan when we were little.' Jeff nodded. 'He used to say Glen and I were John and Michael, and Wendy was Wendy. I always used to ask why he called us Glen and Jeff, in that case.'

'Why did he?'

'Mum. She said John was boring and she used to know a Michael. So here we are.'

'I prefer Glen and Jeff,' said Eve.

'Me too. It didn't help my sister's ego though. Being called Wendy just made her think she was special.'

'Well, she was. She's the only girl,' said Eve before remembering that only a couple of hours earlier she'd thought there were two sisters. 'She is, right?'

'Yeah. There's three of us. And Dad will have split everything as fairly as he could, because that's what he always did. Even though he doesn't need to. Not really.'

'No?'

'No. But he always said I'd get the house. I don't know why.'

Eve caught herself studying Jeff's features.

'Because you look like him,' she murmured under her breath. That was why he seemed so familiar. That was why she'd seen that smile before. His features were littered around the house, in photographs of Stan as a young man. Of course, there were also photos of the children, of Glen, Wendy and Jeff when they were little. Yet, comparing the three of them, Jeff's presence was the one that seemed to resonate within the house.

Jeff searched her eyes and then gave a sad smile.

'Mum used to say that.'

'Jeff?'

They both jumped at Glen's voice and then Jeff's brother appeared in the hallway. He was taller than Jeff, and bulkier, with broader shoulders, something of a belly and brown eyes rimmed red with spent tears. He ran a hand through his dark hair and sighed.

'Wendy's finishing up. You nearly done?' He eyed the boxes and then gave Eve a quick glance.

'Just helping Eve put these in her car and I think I'm all sorted.'

'Those events are cancelled?' Glen asked.

Jeff looked back to Eve and then turned to his brother. Eve silently begged him.

'Yeah,' said Jeff. 'Except the ghost tour. It's tomorrow. It'd be a shame to let those people down.'

Glen struggled for a moment.

'C'mon, Glen,' his brother urged. 'One last

hoorah for Dad. Plus, it's Christmas. Can we really disappoint those people at Christmas?'

Glen rolled his eyes but didn't respond. He only sighed again, crossing his arms. It took Eve a second to realise he was hugging himself. His gaze landed back on her and she snapped her eyes back up to his.

'Dad loved the ghost tours?'

She nodded a little too eagerly.

'He always wanted to make them scarier. We had to hold him back, except on Halloween. We let his imagination run wild then. He practically turned this place into a haunted house. But not at Christmas. It's more of a festive event, looking at the Manor's history with some spooky tales. Think less Exorcist and more Scrooge.'

A smile touched Glen's lips.

'And you lead them round?' he asked her.

'Oh no. I just run it all, in the background really. I have a medium, a psychic, that I hire to lead the tour. She knows the Manor and the stories well now. And Stan used to help me decorate the house. We end in the orchard. We put fairy lights in the trees and hand out mulled wine and mince pies which my friend makes. She's a baker. We were going to have the brass band from the town over to play some carols too.'

Jeff's eyes widened as she spoke.

'That sounds amazing.' He turned to his brother. 'Dad would have loved that.'

Glen's features had softened.

'He would. But Wendy's right. This is our family home. The idea of people traipsing through it talking about ghosts.' He shuddered. 'Could we just do the orchard bit?'

'They've paid for the ghost tour,' said Eve carefully, her mind whirring. 'I guess we could. I'd have to give them some sort of refund though.'

'Or offer to donate the money to charity,' Glen offered.

Eve bristled.

'I think Eve was hoping to pay rent and buy food with that money,' Jeff murmured to his brother.

'Oh. Right.' Glen looked into the cupboard at the remaining boxes. 'We'll think about it,' he told her after a moment's consideration.

Eve hesitated.

'So, I shouldn't cancel it?'

'Not yet,' said Glen.

'No. Just the murder mystery,' said Jeff at the same time.

'Okay.' Eve held back the grin that wanted to beam from her. She could do that. She could run just the one event. That would see her through to January without too much harm done, then she could look into sourcing a new venue.

'We just have to discuss it with Wendy first,' said Glen.

'Oh.' Eve sagged, her hopes dissipating before they'd even fully formed.

5

Eve stopped by the Flour Power Bakery on her way home. Something in the boxes on the back seats rattled as she stopped the car. She slammed the door, locking it behind her as she stepped into the warmth of freshly baked mince pies, hot coffee and friendly chatter. Pausing only to breathe in the aromas, Eve headed straight to the back, saying hello to Pete behind the till as she passed.

'She's in the kitchen,' he called to her. Eve gave him a thumbs up and squeezed past a family crowded around a small table.

'Beth?' Eve entered the kitchen carefully, aware she was bringing her dirty coat and shoes into the food preparation area.

'Eve! How did it go?' Beth appeared, wiping her hands on a towel. She offered Eve an apron but Eve shook her head.

'Sorry. I've got a car full of boxes and bags and I need to go home and cancel things.'

'Oh.' Beth sighed. 'I'm sorry. It didn't go well

then?'

Eve leaned against the wall thoughtfully.

'I don't know. Stan's sons seem lovely. All three of his kids were there, and I say kids, they all seem older than us. Jeff told me to just cancel the murder mystery at New Year's but we'll go ahead with the ghost tour.'

'Really? That's great.' Beth grinned and then stopped. 'Isn't that a bit morbid, given that Stan's only just passed away?'

'Jeff said it would be fitting, his dad would have loved it. And he's right.'

Beth raised an eyebrow.

'And how much did it take to convince him?'

'Oh, no. I didn't. Well, not much. Well, I don't think. He seemed to come to the conclusion on his own. I pointed out it was Christmas and the ghost tour is tomorrow and how sad it would be. Then I ended up telling him about the ghost tours we've done in the past and how good Stan made them and here we are. He changed his mind. But I still have to go cancel the murder mystery. And call Lyn to tell her about Stan. For a psychic, she's not always good at reading the room.'

Beth scoffed at that.

'I wonder why,' she muttered.

'She's not a fake. She's adamant about that,' said Eve, before adding quietly, 'Do you ever wonder if we think she's a fake because believing in her would be too scary?'

'They're all fake, Eve.'

Eve shot Beth a look but didn't have the energy to replay that argument yet again. She'd need a coffee and a lot of chocolate for that one.

'She's a good actress though. She brings a wonderful theatre to it and that's all that Stan ever really wanted. To really spook people.'

'She's definitely spooky.'

Eve ignored that.

'So,' Beth continued, a smirk growing on her lips as she reached for her water bottle. 'Stan's sons are nice, are they?'

Eve smiled before realising what she was doing and stopping herself.

'Yeah, well. Stan was nice, so it stands to reason, doesn't it. Glen – he's the eldest – isn't sure about the ghost tour. But all three had a bit of a fight about the house while I was packing up the car and it sounds like the Manor is going to Jeff. Given his turn around on the ghost tour, that might be good news.' Eve bit her lip as her thoughts raced. 'If I can make this ghost tour amazing, show Jeff just how good it can be, maybe he'll let me keep using the Manor as a venue.'

'That shouldn't be too hard,' said Beth.

'Well. It might. Glen and Wendy aren't happy about the house being used for events.'

'Wendy? Is she Glen's wife?'

'No, their sister. Oh, Beth. I'm not sure about her. I know she's just lost her dad, but she didn't seem happy about Jeff getting the house and Jeff's the only one on my side. Even Glen said they'd have to talk to her first about the ghost tour. She's going to say no.' Eve swallowed on the lump rising in her throat.

'Well, she can't, can she. It's already organised and it's tomorrow night.'

'But it's their house. She could just say no tomorrow and I'd be forced to cancel.' Eve sighed. 'I'd have to refund everyone and still pay Lyn and the brass band. That's too short notice.'

Beth pursed her lips.

'Forget about that. Go with your first plan. Make this ghost tour amazing. I've already baked most of the mince pies. I can do cookies as well, if you like? Gingerbread with icing. Gingerbread Christmas ghosts. We could make little goody bags for them to take home.' Beth's eyes were growing distant, as they always did when she got an idea.

'Sounds amazing,' said Eve. 'Do that. If it all goes to pot, then I'll have them all. Tomorrow evening. By myself. With ice cream and wine.'

Beth gave Eve a look.

'Stop thinking the worst. Go home, get planning and I'll get baking.'

As Eve turned to leave, Beth had a change of heart and asked playfully, 'So, erm, is Jeff or Glen single?'

Eve rolled her eyes.

'Yes. Jeff is. I don't know about Glen. Why? You

want me to set you up?'

'It just occurred to me that this Jeff was all about cancelling these events until he set eyes on you. Then suddenly he changes his mind? Come on.'

Eve caught herself smiling as she replayed their first meeting in her mind.

'No. It wasn't like that. He changed his mind after I told him about the efforts his dad used to go to. He's grieving his father, Beth. That stuff has got to be the furthest from his mind right now.'

'Oh, please. My cousin got together with her husband at a funeral. It's what it does to you. It's like you need to feel something life affirming after such a loss. Imagine, if you fell in love, you wouldn't have to worry about using the house as a venue.'

'I still think Wendy would object, even if we were sisters.'

'No, I meant because you wouldn't need to worry about money.'

'Oh. Oh!' Eve glanced around for something to throw at her friend and although there was nothing to hand, Beth giggled and dodged. 'I wouldn't marry someone just for their house and I wouldn't give up my business if I came into money. Would you give up this bakery if you married someone with money?'

'Absolutely not,' said Beth, still giggling. 'But I notice you haven't objected to the idea of marrying Jeff.'

Eve narrowed her eyes at her friend.

'Is he attractive?' Beth asked, forcing away the giggles.

Eve smiled at her.

'He wouldn't like me.'

'Pfft. Of course he would.'

'I took the hats to the car by piling them on my head.'

Beth stopped giggling and stood still, staring at her friend.

'Oh, Eve. If he didn't fall madly in love with you in that moment then he doesn't deserve you.' Beth snorted. 'Wish I'd seen it.'

'And you didn't tell me I had icing sugar in my hair when I left. Jeff thought it was fake snow.'

Beth laughed.

'That was the first conclusion he came to? You're made for each other.'

The two women grinned at one another and then Eve noticed the tray of mince pies waiting on the side.

'I'm taking one of these. In compensation for you thinking I would marry for money. Just be glad I'm not throwing this at you.' She took a bite of the mince pie, still warm from the oven, and gave a little moan of pleasure. 'These are so good.'

Beth said nothing but she didn't need to, her expression and the light in her eyes said it all.

'See you tomorrow,' said Eve around her mouthful. Beth waved to her and Eve walked back into the main part of the bakery, leaving the sound of Beth's laughter behind her.

Once home, Eve dithered about whether to leave the boxes and bags of murder mystery props and costumes in the car or whether to take them upstairs to her flat. After weighing up her options and testing the weight of one of the boxes, she decided to leave them for the time being, or until she could bribe some friends to help her. Once in her flat, she chucked her keys into the little bowl on the side, slid out of her coat, turned the heating on and did the customary dance to warm up while making cold noises. In the kitchen, she filled the kettle and turned it on, and then Eve stopped.

Her mind swam, from painful jolts in her chest at the memories of Stan and the thought of never seeing him again to wondering what the future held for the event business she loved so much. As her breathing grew shallow, Eve sat on her kitchen floor, hugging her knees to her chest, and she let the tears come. The sobs wracked through her body, her nose running and she let out wails of grief as they washed over her.

Once the crying had subsided and the kettle clicked to say it was boiled, Eve picked herself up and found a box of tissues to clean and dry her face. With a steaming cup of tea and feeling a little lighter, Eve sat on her sofa and pulled her laptop over. She would have to cancel the murder mystery event first, then she would need to call Lyn and Bob, her brass band contact, to update them. In theory, the ghost tour was planned and ready to go, but Eve would double check everything that night. Then, she should go to bed.

That was her plan and it had been a good plan, except that when she finally did fall into bed, after more tears and awkward phone calls and curling up to feel sorry for herself, she just couldn't sleep.

Every time she closed her eyes, they pinged back open and her mind swam from one thought to the next. Soon, her memories of Stan were merging with those of meeting his children earlier that day. His stature merging with Wendy's, his hair with Glen's, his eyes with Jeff's. Eve found herself picking apart the new memories of Jeff, matching his smile and tone to his father's. Eve would miss Stan's laugh, his excitement, his sense of fun, and then her mind pushed the vision of Jeff to her. The man who might give her some hope this Christmas, the man who might give her hope next year, if only she could impress him enough with this one event.

After closing her eyes and fidgeting, Eve groaned and sat up, turning on the light. Reaching for a notebook and pen, she rearranged her pillows and started jotting down notes. Soon, she was out of bed putting the kettle on again and opening her laptop, surrounding herself with pieces of paper full of scribbles with ideas of events, memories of Stan and plans for the future.

6

Eve groaned awkwardly as she woke. Pain ripped through her back and arms. She sighed to herself as she realised the position she was in, draped across the sofa, shivering gently, bent at an odd angle with one arm pinned behind her head. As she righted herself and sat up, paper fell off the sofa around her and she shot out a hand to save her empty mug from falling off the table. At least she'd finally managed to get some sleep. Blinking to clear her vision, Eve picked up the papers, trying to decipher the notes. Then she frowned. What was that noise? Something vibrating against wood.

Eyes wide, Eve cleared her table in one sweep and found her phone underneath a sheath of papers. She recognised the number immediately.

'Hello?' She held the phone away and coughed. 'Hello?' she repeated in a clearer voice.

'Eve? It's Jeff Hargreaves.'

Eve's heart began pounding.

'Hi,' she managed.

'Hi. Sorry, I know it's early. But I didn't know how much time you needed. We're good to go ahead with the ghost tour tonight. Erm, do you need anything from us? From me, I mean, I'll be the only one here. Along with Janine. Glen and Wendy have gone home. So it's just us. So, what do we do now? How does this work?'

Grinning, Eve silently punched the air and then took a second to regain her composure.

'That's wonderful news, thank you so much. You don't need to do anything. I'll need to come over early and set everything up, make sure everything and everyone's in place. Jan can help me, she already knows where everything goes.'

'Oh. Okay. I mean, I'd like to help, if I can. What did my dad used to do?'

A shot of pleasure twisted through Eve's gut.

'That would be great, if you don't mind. He'd help with the decorating where he could but mostly he was the ideas man. He'd sit back and boss us around and—' Eve paused, realising what she'd just said.

Jeff gave something of a sad laugh.

'Don't worry. This is your thing. I won't be doing any bossing around.'

'Thanks,' said Eve. 'I mean it. Thank you, for letting us go ahead. I know this is a really difficult time. Losing your dad at Christmas is bad enough without having me in your way. So I really appreciate you doing this.'

There was a long pause on the phone and Eve began to wonder if Jeff had gone. Had the connection cut out? She opened her mouth to see if he was still there when he spoke.

'I think it'll be fun,' he said and there was a slight crack in his voice that tore at Eve. 'Dad would have wanted it to go ahead.'

Eve nodded and then realised Jeff couldn't see her.

'Are you okay?' she said before clenching her eyes shut. What a stupid thing to ask. 'I mean, you know, if you want to talk, about anything, I'm a fairly unbiased ear. I'm happy to listen.'

'That's very kind of you, to offer free therapy, but I'm all right.'

'Okay. Look,' continued Eve without thinking. 'If you need a break today or over Christmas in general, my friend owns a bakery on the high street. Flour Power Bakery. She does the best mince pies and cakes and coffee. And I'm often down there, so if you do ever fancy a chat.'

She could almost hear Jeff smiling.

'Thanks,' he said. 'I'll bear that in mind. So, what time will you be coming today?'

'I'll be there around two this afternoon. Is that okay? People start arriving after dark, around half five. We get going at six. It'll all be over by eight.'

'Wow. I can even have an early night.'

Eve laughed.

'That's the beauty of winter ghost tours.'

There was another pause and this time Eve waited.

'Be honest, are there really ghosts in this house?'

Eve hesitated, wondering how he would react to the truth.

'Honestly? I guess it depends on how you define ghosts.'

Jeff barked a laugh.

'Not sure I deserved the philosophical answer but thanks anyway. See you later.'

'See you. And thanks again.'

Jeff hung up and Eve lowered her phone, staring at the screen. Then she jumped up and screamed, 'Yes!' at the top of her voice, her arms in the air. Giggling, she danced into her bathroom and had a quick hot shower before pulling on layers of warm clothes, trapping in the heat, grabbing her bag and coat, and slamming the door behind her.

'It's on!' she yelled as she walked into Flour Power Bakery. 'Beth?'

Beth appeared from below the counter, making Eve jump.

'Don't do that,' she said, hand over her heart as Beth grinned.

'It's not my fault that you walk in while I'm down there.'

'Really? Because sometimes it feels like you see me coming and you hide.'

Beth made a noise as if that couldn't possibly be true but that smile was still on her lips.

A couple sitting in the corner grinned at them as Eve undid her coat.

'What's on?' Beth asked. 'Coffee?'

'Please. I haven't had any breakfast. I fell asleep on my sofa last night while working. I know, I know,' she added when Beth gave her a look. 'I couldn't sleep. And they say you should get up and do something when you can't sleep.'

'Do something like read a book, not worry about your business,' said Beth. 'And then go back to bed when you're feeling sleepy.'

Eve waved her words away with exaggerated gestures.

'Whatever. I'll have a coffee, yes, thank you. And the ghost tour is on. Jeff called me this morning, woke me up in fact, and told me it's on. We're on!' Eve gave a little squeal and then was instantly distracted by the cakes in the display case by the till. 'You made sugar biscuits.'

'I did. First thing. They're fresh, I only just put them out, and no you can't have a sugar biscuit for breakfast. I'll make you some toast with eggs, if you like?'

'How about pancakes? Your pancakes are incredible.'

'Eggs on toast it is,' said Beth, placing Eve's coffee on the counter and disappearing into the kitchen. 'Grab a table,' she called over her shoulder.

Eve took one by the window. The bakery hadn't had a chance to steam up yet so she had a perfectly clear view of the high street, the cars moving past and the odd early morning shopper or person on their way to work.

Pete appeared from the kitchen and greeted Eve.

'I hear the ghost tour is back on?' he asked her, taking his place behind the till.

'It is.'

'Sort of wish I'd bought tickets now. Are you sold out?'

'Yeah. Sorry. I would say maybe next time but...' Eve shrugged.

'You'll find somewhere better,' he told her. 'You know, you should branch out. Offer your services elsewhere. What about that old medieval jail that's over there somewhere.' He pointed to his right. 'I'm always seeing signs for it but never been. A ghost tour in a medieval jail. Think about that.'

Eve did think about it, immediately her brain took the idea and began running through the possibilities. She'd never wanted to start a ghost tour business, she'd just enjoyed running events.

'Maybe,' she said as the door opened and a family of four came in, bringing a gust of cold air with them. 'Thanks. Good idea.'

Pete gave her a nod before turning his attention to the family. Eve went back to staring out of the window, sipping at her coffee. Maybe she could follow the ghost tour ideas, but that would probably mean believing a little more in the paranormal. Perhaps this was an opportunity to try something new. She narrowed her eyes as her mind whirred and then started as Beth placed a couple of plates piled with toast and poached eggs on the table. She sat opposite Eve and then stared at her friend.

'What? What are you thinking now?'

Eve realised she was looking suspiciously at Beth.

'You've always been a good cook,' she murmured.

Beth sat back.

'Yeah?' she said cautiously.

'Have you ever thought about cooking for dinner parties?'

'Yup.'

'And?'

'Nope.'

Eve sighed.

'Look, I know our passions can intertwine sometimes and that's wonderful,' said Beth, cutting into her toast and egg, the yolk spilling out. 'But that doesn't mean we should go into business together. We've talked about this.'

'Yeah, I know,' said Eve, picking up her knife and fork. 'But what if we weren't in business together? What if I hired you? To cater at parties. Ooh, at weddings!'

Beth watched her friend's animated features and smiled as she swallowed her mouthful.

'You want to become a wedding planner? That's quite a difference from murder mysteries and ghost hunts.'

'Yeah.' Eve pushed her egg and then sliced into it, watching the yolk run out in a glorious mess. 'You know what scares me?'

'What?'

'What if Stan had all the good ideas? What if, without him, I'm just good at organising where and when people should be without making the event actually good?'

Beth considered Eve as they tucked into the breakfasts.

'You learned a lot from Stan,' she said. 'And you had incredible ideas before he came into your life. Just imagine what you'll be capable of now.'

Eve's eyes filled up. She blinked the tears back, sniffed and filled her mouth with toast and runny egg.

The door to the bakery opened, sending another waft of cold air over them. Eve swallowed hard as Jeff walked in and approached the counter. He took off gloves as he talked to Pete.

'That's Jeff,' Eve hissed. Beth looked back over her shoulder just as Pete pointed them out to Jeff, who turned to look at them. Beth turned back sharply, raising her eyebrows at Eve.

'Cute,' she mouthed.

Eve gave her a warning look.

Jeff wandered over, his eyes on Eve.

'Hi. You decided to come check this place out?' Eve asked, smiling up at him.

'Yeah. Thought it might be good to get out.' Jeff looked around the bakery. 'When I was a kid, this was a haberdashery.'

'Ha! Yeah. It was when I bought it. The planning permission was fun, I can tell you,' said Beth. 'I'm Beth.' She held out a hand.

'Jeff Hargreaves.' Jeff shook her hand, glancing at Eve who was searching for the right words.

'Lovely to meet you. I'm so sorry about your father. He was a wonderful man. I always made extra mince pies for him. I used to sneak them to him when Eve and Jan weren't looking.'

Eve looked at her friend.

'Did you? I never knew that.'

'I'm very good at being sneaky,' said Beth. She stood up as Eve ate her last mouthful of breakfast. Beth took her plate. 'I'll let you two talk,' she said, giving Eve an encouraging look. Eve ignored her.

'I'm just getting a coffee to takeaway,' said Jeff.

'Pete'll bring it over when it's ready,' said Beth, gesturing to the chair she'd vacated.

Jeff sat down and they watched as Beth bustled into the kitchen at the back.

'She seems nice.'

'She's all right. I mostly stick around for the cake,' said Eve, smiling as Jeff looked at her. 'We've been friends since university,' she clarified with a shrug. 'Sometimes she knows me better than I know myself.' She stopped and considered those words, glancing up at Jeff with new eyes. He didn't notice. 'You don't recognise her? She grew up around here too. I only moved here about five years ago. There's only the one high school here, right?'

Jeff fidgeted and it took Eve a moment to recognise it as embarrassment.

'We were shipped off to private school. We didn't venture down here often. Sometimes, Mum would take me into the shops, but usually only around Christmas.' He breathed in and closed his eyes. 'I can smell mince pies.'

'It always smells of fresh mince pies in here, from November to the end of the year.'

Jeff and Eve looked into each other's eyes, both smiling. Just as it occurred to Eve that, while the silence wasn't awkward, perhaps someone should speak, Pete placed a takeaway cup of coffee down in front of Jeff.

'Thanks.' Jeff began to pull his gloves back on and a hint of panic flittered through Eve.

'So, erm, where do you live now?' she asked.

Jeff sat back.

'London. I run an architectural firm.'

'Really? You're an architect?'

'I am. I think that's why Dad wanted me to have the house. I think he thought I'd appreciate it more. Although I'm not sure how true that is.'

'You don't like the house?'

Jeff appeared shocked.

'No. I adore it. It's beautiful and old and home. It's just that both Wendy and Glen have families.

Shouldn't a house like that be filled with warmth and laughter and children?'

Eve fought against a smile and distracted herself with the last of her coffee.

'Oh, I don't know. It sounds like a nice place for a fun uncle to live.'

Jeff laughed.

'And a nice place to start a family,' he murmured.

'Is that the plan?'

Jeff shrugged.

'It always was. I just can't seem to find anyone to start one with. Dating's hard. Don't you think?'

Eve nodded, trying to remember the last date she'd been on.

'I'm beginning to think that the right woman for me doesn't live in London,' Jeff continued. 'I get the feeling I've been looking in the wrong places.'

'I know what you mean,' Eve murmured. Jeff looked up into her eyes. 'I mean, you get to a certain age and you have to start wondering if your dream man, or woman, even exists.'

Jeff grinned.

'What's the dream man then?'

Eve chose her next words carefully.

'The usual,' she said. 'Attractive, charming, intelligent, great sense of humour.'

'I think quite a few of them exist?'

'Yeah, but none have been quite right so far. Go on then, what's the dream woman?'

'Fun,' said Jeff. 'I want someone I can have fun

with. Someone a bit different.'

Eve softened.

'Yeah. Someone that's just a touch quirky.'

'Exactly.'

'Who you can have in-jokes with but also serious conversations,' Eve added.

'Yes. Who likes hugging. I like hugging.'

'Me too. And staying in and watching a movie.'

'With popcorn.'

Eve and Jeff stopped and searched one another's eyes.

'Someone who likes Christmas,' Eve murmured.

'Someone who'll stay up and look at the stars, just in case,' Jeff added.

Eve's heart was pounding, her mouth dry, but she couldn't take her eyes from Jeff. He didn't move, his blue eyes soft, a smile playing on his lips.

The door to the bakery opened and this time the wind pushed the cold air in. Everyone in the bakery complained until the door was shut. Jeff shivered and pulled his coat tighter around his neck.

'I'd best be going,' he said, standing up and taking his coffee. 'See you this afternoon?'

'With bells on,' Eve murmured. Jeff glanced back to her curiously and she mentally shook herself. 'Two o'clock. See you then.'

7

'Merry Christmas Eve Eve!' Janine cried, leaving the house with open arms as Eve got out of the car. Eve grinned and let Stan's old housekeeper embrace her in a tight bear hug. Janine was approaching her late sixties and seemed to have an apron for every occasion. She was rarely straight faced and always a little flushed. Her silvery dark hair was usually tied back in a mess of a bun, mostly to keep it out of the food she prepared. Janine loved a clean house but she was the first to admit that she was at her happiest in a kitchen playing with and making something delicious. Her breads were quite famous amongst her friends and she'd even taught Beth a few things. Eve hugged her back, breathing in the scent of roast beef in her hair.

'You're cooking,' she said, her voice muffled by Janine's hair and coat.

'Indeed I am. Roast beef pastry parcels and festive sausage rolls. With vegan options.' Janine pulled away, her eyes brimming with tears and that was when Eve noticed how red the woman's eyes were. She took Janine's hand and squeezed it.

'I'm so sorry, Jan.'

Janine tried to smile but her chin quivered. The tears fell down her cheeks.

'Oh, blast.' Producing a crumpled tissue from her pocket, she wiped at her eyes. 'I thought I was done with this.'

'I don't think we'll be done with it for a while,' Eve told her. 'You need to let it out.'

Janine nodded.

'How are you holding up?' she asked.

Eve looked up at the house.

'Okay, I think. I don't think it'll hit me until after tonight. Hopefully not during tonight.'

Janine followed her gaze up to the house.

'I was so pleased that Jeff is letting you go through with the ghost hunt. It was always my favourite. Stan would have been happy about that. Although I can almost hear him chastising Jeff about not having the murder mystery, can't you? Anyway, the house is cleaned and some of the decorations are up. It's surprisingly difficult knowing where things go without Stan telling me what to do.' Janine sniffed. 'Do you want to take a look?'

Eve nodded and began to follow her into the house.

'What do you think of Jeff?' Janine whispered over her shoulder.

Eve sighed.

'He seems nice. Is he here?'

'Yes. He was sorting through boxes when I started decorating. He offered to help but he was more useless than I am. I think we both need some direction from you.' Janine held the door open for Eve and shut it behind them, gesturing to the grand staircase. 'He's up there. Shall we go find him? I know he'd love to help.'

Eve took a moment to breathe in the scents of the tall pine tree, the chill that comes from trying to heat such a large house, and the ever-present smell of polish. The delicious warm aromas of roasting beef and spices came through from the kitchen and Eve's stomach rumbled despite having just polished off a mini chocolate yule log made by Beth.

'Yes, let's get decorating,' she said, shrugging off her coat. Janine took it from her, snatching it when Eve went to protest.

'I'll put these away and come find you upstairs. You go find Jeff. He's probably in his father's study. I left the box of decorations with him. Lord only knows where he's put that large spider.' Janine walked away, humming to herself and Eve watched for a moment, wondering what the woman's plans were after Christmas was over. Maybe Eve could convince her to go into the party planning business as Beth wasn't keen.

Eve walked up the stairs, her hand trailing on the banister, watching the tree as she rose up until she could almost touch the angel on the top. She paused for a moment, feeling Stan's presence, and then continued on. The landing was bright and airy, certainly not good enough for a ghost tour. Eve checked in on the rooms that were used during the tour and left those doors open, closing the others, until she reached Stan's study. Inside, Jeff was sitting at his father's desk leafing through a book. She knocked gently on the door and Jeff looked up, smiling as his vision focused on her.

'Happy Christmas Eve Eve, Eve,' he said, grinning.

For a moment, Eve was taken aback.

'Sorry, I bet you get that all the time at this time of year,' said Jeff, placing the book down on the desk. Eve didn't get a chance to correct him. He looked around, inhaling deeply. 'I always loved this room when I was little. Dad used to read in here with me. Some days I'd play with my Lego on the floor while he was working.'

'Oh? You were an architect from an early age then?'

Jeff lovingly caressed the arms of the chair he was sitting on.

'According to Dad, I was always building something. Out of blocks, Lego, snow, sand, mashed potato.'

Eve smiled.

'This has always been my favourite room,' she murmured. 'There's something particularly cosy about it.'

'Especially with the fire lit,' Jeff agreed. 'I'm making this my own study and library, so it won't be changing. I'll just be adding more books.'

Eve blinked and looked away as Jeff caught her studying him.

'What would you do?' he asked. 'If this place was yours?'

Eve paused, wondering if she'd heard him right.

'You mean, if I was you?'

'No. If you were you but you'd inherited this place. What would you do with it? Would you live here?'

'Of course,' she said, without hesitation. Jeff smiled. Eve considered the rest of her response. 'I'd live here, but I'd also hold events here. But then, that's my business, isn't it. And I'd sell my friend's cakes and things here during the events. But it'd be a family home too, because that's what it should be. A home, filled with warmth and laughter and love. And cake,' she added.

Jeff watched her, still smiling.

'That sounds wonderful.'

'Really? Even the business part?'

Jeff nodded, glancing down at his father's desk.

'I guess I could move my firm up here. Or at least have another office here. I don't fancy splitting my time between here and London.'

Eve's shoulders dropped. So that was why he'd asked. He was trying to work out whether to live in the house or go back to London. Eve couldn't

65

imagine not living in the Manor if you owned it.

'Jan said you might want to help with the decorating?' she asked.

'Oh, yes.' Jeff jumped up and walked around the desk. 'I had a go but didn't have a clue what to do. I thought I'd best leave it to the professional.'

'It just takes a bit of practise, that's all,' she told him as he fetched the box. 'We need to put up some cobwebs. Jan keeps this place too clean. And there's a giant spider. Where's the giant spider?'

'In the bedroom.' Jeff pushed past Eve and led her down the hallway, opening a door to the left where Eve hadn't checked yet. Inside was a double bed facing the wall and on top of the covers was a giant, furry black spider. 'I thought he needed a rest,' Jeff added.

Eve laughed.

'He was very busy a couple of months ago for Halloween,' she admitted, walking inside and picking the spider up. 'He goes on one of the doors, in the shadows. Stan managed to get him to move at the just right moment on Halloween and made a woman scream.'

Jeff grinned.

'Dad and his pranks.'

Eve began to unpack the box of decorations and walk Jeff through the ghost tour, telling him where to place the cobwebs and just how to position a witch in the corner, by the window. Janine came up to help and soon she was putting the finishing touches to the house as Eve instructed Jeff where to put the lights. It was dusk by the time they finished, the shadows growing longer around the house.

Jeff turned on the Christmas lights, alongside the glowing ghost tour ones, and began playing some low Christmas music as Eve welcomed Lyn the psychic.

'All done,' said Jeff, approaching Eve and Lyn.

'Great. Thanks. Jeff, this is Lyn, she leads the ghost tours.'

'Jeff,' said Lyn, taking his hand before he'd fully outstretched it and shaking it hard. 'I'm so sorry about your father. Stan was a wonderful man.'

'Thanks.' Jeff took his hand back. 'Do you run many ghost tours?'

'Oh, yes.' Lyn held up her chin proudly. 'I mostly do séances and readings, but I do love a good ghost tour. I wonder what we'll find tonight. Perhaps Stan will come to say hello. Are those beef pastries I smell?' Lyn wandered off towards the kitchen and there came the raised voices of excited women as she found Janine.

'Well, that's it,' said Eve. 'Beth will arrive later with the mince pies and she and Jan will get the brass band into place. Just need the customers to arrive now. They'll come in dribs and drabs, so we'll need to make sure the food and drinks are ready.'

'They eat first?'

'We offer them the treats Jan's prepared along with a little glass of wine or juice when they arrive.

Just until everyone's here and it's dark enough to start.'

Jeff nodded, distracted.

'Are you okay?' Eve asked. 'You don't have to stick around if you'd rather have some time alone. You know the route, so you can go and hide if you prefer?'

'Oh, no. No. I'd love to be involved. At least to follow on the tour, if that's okay?'

'Of course.' Eve resisted the urge to reach out to him, despite how much her instincts screamed at her to touch his arm comfortingly.

'I dreamt about him last night,' said Jeff after a moment, his voice low, his gaze on the Christmas tree.

'About your father?'

Jeff nodded.

'We were here, standing here, and he was happy.' Jeff smiled. 'I woke up and sobbed my eyes out.' He sighed.

This time Eve's instincts acted before she could stop them. She reached out and brushed her hand against his, taking it and squeezing. Jeff looked down at their hands and then up at her, his eyes rimmed red.

She smiled and went to take her hand away but Jeff held it tightly.

'I see now why you were important to him,' he murmured. 'Thank you, for bringing him all this joy, right up until the end.'

Eve's nose stung as her eyes filled.

Jeff dropped her hand quickly as there came a knock at the front door.

'Oh.' Eve wiped at her eyes. 'They're here. We're starting. Can you go tell Jan?'

Jeff left without saying anything and Eve turned to the front door, taking a deep breath. It was time to put away thoughts of grief and what should have been. There was a ghost tour to run.

8

Within half an hour, everyone had arrived and the
Manor was filled with a warm glow, gentle chatter
and laughter against the backdrop of the soft music.
Lyn stepped forward and turned the music off
before tapping on her glass with her long fingernails.

'Ladies and gentlemen!' She waited until the
chatter had quietened and she had everyone's
attention. 'We're about to begin. Please place your
glasses on a table near you and gather at the bottom
of the stairs.'

There was movement as the group did as they
were told and Lyn positioned herself on the stairs.
Eve found Jeff and, giving him a warm smile,
positioned them so that they took up the rear of the
group. Janine turned off some of the lights, creating
a stir of murmurs in the group. Jeff flinched,
looking around the hall. He took a shuddering
breath as Lyn began.

'This manor house was built in the late eighteenth century but it stands on the foundations of something much older. Records show that this land once belonged to a monastery and the remains of a chapel have been found in the grounds. Naturally there are tales of spirits of the monks who once called that monastery home being spotted in the grounds, mostly going about their duties but sometimes watching those pottering about the gardens. We'll talk more about them later, when we head outside.

'Since the manor house was built upon the land sold by the church, a number of families have lived here. As with all families, there have been a fair share of secrets and scandal, leading up to the current owners, the Hargreaves family, the patriarch of which sadly passed away only days ago. Stanley Hargreaves loved these tours.' Lyn paused to close her eyes. 'I am sure you will all join me in sending our love and deepest sympathies to his family and friends who have lost a wonderful man. And we reach out to Stanley, if he is still among us, to invite him to join us on this tour tonight. Just for once, to become part of that which he enjoyed so much.'

Eve glanced up at Jeff, unsure whether Lyn's words were in poor taste or not. Jeff didn't react, keeping his eyes on Lyn. Eve looked back to the stairs, wondering if she would catch the outline of Stan on the steps behind Lyn. There was nothing there but shadows.

Lyn spoke a little more of what to expect, building the tension further, before asking the group to follow her up the stairs.

The group moved silently and Eve fell into old habits, watching those in front of her peering into the shadows, making each other jump as they brushed shoulders and laughing nervously. Lyn's voice faded as Eve watched the group enjoying themselves, until Jeff flinched, catching Eve's attention.

'This bedroom was also the room belonging to a young woman who fell madly in love with a wealthy man from the city. He promised to marry her and their ceremony was arranged in the local church for Christmas Eve. On the day of the wedding, our young bride put on her gown and travelled excitedly to meet her groom surrounded by family and friends. The groom never turned up. Thinking he had fallen out of love with her, she ran all the way back to this house and shut herself away in her room. She refused to eat or drink, she wouldn't speak to anyone or let anyone into the room. She died of a broken heart surrounded by these four walls, her door locked from the inside. Her groom-to-be, however, died on his way to his wedding when the horses pulling his carriage spooked on a bridge, the carriage capsizing and throwing our young groom into the water where he drowned. You might hope that their spirits would meet in the afterlife, but every Christmas weeping can be heard from this empty room, as our young bride returns to mourn what could have been.'

The group silently appraised the bedroom and then followed Lyn further down the hallway.

'Is that true? I don't remember that story,' Jeff whispered.

Eve only gave him a smile and followed the group, unaware that Jeff was no longer behind her.

It was only when Jeff had caught her up that she noticed he'd been missing for those few seconds. She took his arm, trying to gauge how he was feeling.

There was a scream as a motion sensitive light flicked on, illuminating the giant spider on the next door. Eve resisted the urge to cackle. Jeff started, his hand gripping Eve's arm and pulling her back. She glanced up to him as his nerves calmed.

'You put that there,' she murmured. 'Remember?'

Jeff gave a nervous laugh.

'This room leads up to the attic, long since locked and never reopened. Beyond the door is where it is rumoured a witch once lived, casting spells over those who lived in the town, granting them one Christmas wish each. But each wish came with a cost. So it was that one cold December evening, someone came to knock on her door.'

Eve nearly yelped when a grip closed on her wrist and pulled her back. She looked up into Jeff's eyes, his skin paling.

'Are you okay?' She frowned, concern etched into her features as she studied him. 'You don't look okay. Is this too much?'

'Are they real?' he asked, speaking too fast. 'The ghost stories. About this place?' he hissed.

Eve looked back to the group to make sure they couldn't hear her and then led Jeff away, back towards the stairs, just in case.

'No,' she told him. 'I mean, that woman did exist and her groom did die on the way to the wedding, but she knew and she mourned, and went on to marry someone else. I think she was from the first family to live here. The family that built this house. We adapted it and added the bit about the Christmas wedding. And there was never a witch who lived in the attic granting Christmas wishes for an awful cost until her true love came back for her one Christmas. That one was your dad's idea. There was a chapel and monastery here though. Those stories are reportedly true but I've personally never seen anything and neither did your dad.'

Jeff exhaled long and deep.

'So, this house isn't haunted?'

'No. Lyn just tells a good story. I'm sorry. This was a bad idea. I shouldn't have let you tag along. I should have known it might freak you out. Come on, let's go downstairs and chat with Jan over a mince pie. See if Beth's here with the band.' Eve went to go down the stairs.

'Only, I saw my dad.'

Eve stopped and turned back to Jeff.

'Excuse me?'

'In the bedroom. When everyone else had carried on. He stood in front of me and he smiled and then he looked at you. He looked at peace.' Jeff's eyes glistened with unspent tears. 'Do you think I'm crazy?'

Eve was silent for a moment, her mouth open.

'Of course not,' she murmured, searching for the right comforting words. 'Lots of people say that they sense their loved ones after they've passed on. Maybe he came to say goodbye.'

Jeff nodded and rubbed at his eyes with a thumb.

The tour was coming back down the hallway, heading for the stairs and outside to continue the ghost stories out in the gardens. Eve and Jeff stood to the side and let them pass. The group was quiet but in the dim light, Eve could make out the smirks and sparkling eyes. She exhaled slowly. They were having a good time. At least there was that.

Once the group had passed, Eve turned back to Jeff. He appeared thoughtful, then he strode past her, opening the door to his father's study and wandering inside, behind the desk to the window. Eve followed slowly.

'Do you believe in ghosts?' he asked, his back to Eve.

'I believe in something,' she admitted. 'But I'm not quite sure what.'

'What if Dad is haunting the house?' Jeff asked

quietly.

'Would that be a bad thing?' Eve mused, stepping further into the study and wondering if she could turn the lights on. The shadows flickered from the spooky lights placed in the hallway and the emotion coming off Jeff in waves was making her see things that weren't there. A lengthening shadow, a flash of light that couldn't exist, the door moving ever so slightly on its own.

'It would mean he had unfinished business, wouldn't it.' Jeff turned to look at her, his cheeks wet with tears.

All thoughts of shadows and doors moving went out of Eve's head and she walked over to Jeff, using her sleeve over her thumb to wipe his tears away.

'Your father was a happy man,' she told him in a loud voice to dispel the mood. 'He was loved and he loved. He had fun and he ate what he wanted and he said things how he saw them. What business could he possibly have left unfinished?'

Jeff nodded, his brows knitting into a frown as he thought.

'Apart from turning this into a real ghost tour,' he suggested with a weak attempt at a laugh. A chill ran through Eve and she echoed the laugh.

'Nah. He wouldn't do that. He knew ghosts terrified me. He liked a prank and spooking people but actually scaring them? No. Did you feel scared when you saw him?'

'No,' Jeff admitted. 'Although...' He looked into

Eve's eyes. 'There was something strange about the way he looked after you as you walked away.'

'Oh, don't say that,' said Eve, wrapping her arms around herself.

'He looked at you with love but also...'

'Also?' Eve encouraged, wondering how on earth Jeff would finish that sentence.

Jeff searched her eyes again, his own softening, and then, infuriatingly, he shrugged.

'I don't know. It doesn't matter. Come on. They're outside now, let's go join them.' Jeff walked away, out of the room and Eve listened to his thumping footsteps on the stairs. She remained behind Stan's desk in his study, unable to move, wondering what had just happened.

She glanced about the dark room.

'Stan?' she said, loud enough that she was sure all the shadows could hear her. 'If you're there, if you can hear me, please don't haunt this house. Please be at peace. And what was Jeff trying to say?' she added quietly to herself.

There came a bang and Eve squealed, her heart pounding. Her hand automatically going to her chest to calm herself, she carefully made her way across the room where a framed photo had fallen from the wall. Gingerly, she picked up the photo. It was black and white showing Stan posing with his wife, his arm around her waist, grinning like a man who had everything he needed in the world. They weren't as young as Eve had expected. Stan was perhaps in his late thirties although his wife could have been in her late twenties. She appeared giddy, her smile broad and her cheeks flushed. Eve couldn't help but smile back at them, feeling the love coming off the photo.

'You're with her now, aren't you? I hope you are,' she murmured. Turning the picture over so she could see how to hang it back up, Eve stopped. On the back of the frame, written in large letters with what looked like a fine marker pen, were the words, Everything You Need Is Right In Front Of You.

A sob wrenched through Eve, surprising her. With trembling hands, holding back the tears, she hung the photo back up and smiled again at Stan and his wife.

'I hope one day I'm as happy and in love as you were,' she told him. 'I miss you so much already. Thank you for passing your fun gene onto your son,' she added, thinking of Jeff's smile and the twinkle in his eyes.

As she turned to leave, there was another thump. Eve slowly turned back to face the room, terrified that she would come face to face with Stan's spirit.

No. It was another framed photo falling from the wall. Frowning, Eve picked it up and glanced at the picture. There were no words on the back this time but the photo was of Stan's three children. Glen, standing tall and proud over his siblings, Wendy grinning stupidly for the camera, and young Jeff, sticking his tongue out. Eve grinned in a half laugh, hanging the picture back up and pausing to stare at the young Jeff. The resemblance to his father was uncanny, even from such an early age. Her gaze lingered as her body turned and she left the room, heading towards the stairs, the smile still on her lips.

9

Eve walked out into the chill of the dark evening and joined the end of the tour group as they wandered past. Jeff was trailing behind, a thoughtful expression in his eyes and brow. Eve's stomach twisted as she caught sight of him. It made her hesitate as the tingles spread through her body but then Jeff caught sight of her and she didn't have the time to work out what those feelings meant.

'There you are.' He waited for her as the group headed towards the orchard. 'Where did you go?'

'I was still in the study. Something weird happened,' said Eve, catching him up.

'Oh?'

'A photo fell off the wall. Of your mum and dad. Stan had written a message on the back.'

Jeff stopped walking and stared at her.

'What did it say?'

'Everything you need is right in front of you,' Eve quoted. 'Very romantic. He really did love your mum. Whenever he would talk about her, I would wish that I'd find someone one day who loved me as much as he loved her.'

Jeff smiled.

'Yeah. Well. You didn't live with them. Kissing and cuddling all the time. It was disgusting.'

Eve laughed.

'Really? You don't want that?'

Jeff's gaze lingered on her and Eve's stomach flipped again.

'Oh, definitely. I just didn't want that when I was a kid. It was embarrassing back then. Now I'm proud of them for being that affectionate with each other.' He looked past Eve and up at the house behind her. 'Everything you need is right in front of you,' he murmured.

Eve followed his eyes to the house.

'Do you think that's true?' When she turned back, she reeled to find Jeff staring intently at her.

'I do,' he murmured, his gaze travelling down her body before he sharply turned and strode to catch up with the tour group.

Breathing hard, Eve followed at a slower pace to give herself some time to think. If she didn't know better, she could have sworn that Jeff was attracted to her. She'd been wrong about these things in the past, so it probably meant nothing, especially as he was grieving his father. Given her own physical reactions, did she find Jeff attractive?

She studied him as she caught up, moving to stand beside him at the entrance to the small orchard. It was a square patch of land planted with apple and pear trees, enclosed by hedge and an open fence to allow wildlife in and out. Of all the grounds, this was Eve's favourite. It was also the favourite spot of the local bat population who swooped around the trees at dusk before the insects gravitated towards what light emanated from the house.

Now, the orchard was festooned with twinkling fairy lights. There was a rose arch wrapped in lights at the end of the orchard and around it were the brass band. As Lyn finished her talk and pointed out the table of warm mince pies, gingerbread ghosts and mulled wine off to the side, the band struck up with a gentle rendition of Silent Night.

Eve inhaled slowly. The air was heavy, filled with the scent of mud, bare trees, an open sky and the waft of the wine, pies and gingerbread. If she wasn't mistaken, the scent of snow hung in the air, bringing up wonderful cosy childhood memories. It was only then that Eve realised she'd forgotten to grab her coat on the way out. She hugged herself, giving a little shiver. Then, without warning, her shoulders were warm. She looked up to find Jeff placing his coat around her.

'What idiot comes out here on Christmas Eve Eve without a coat,' he chastised gently, his eyes twinkling in the fairy lights. Eve's breath caught in her throat.

'Won't you be cold?'

Jeff shrugged.

'I'll let you know when I am and you can give it me back.' He gave her a wink and then walked over to the mince pies.

Eve suppressed an involuntary giggle at the wink and watched him go. Over his shoulder, Beth caught her eye. There was no way Jeff wouldn't have seen the look on Beth's face and Eve's pulse raced at the thought.

'That went very well, I think. A couple of people have already been over to ask me questions,' said Lyn at Eve's shoulder. Eve nodded, not taking her eyes from Jeff's back. 'It's such a shame it'll be our last one.'

With those words, Eve deflated, her attention ripped from Jeff and onto Lyn.

'It is, isn't it,' she murmured.

'Stan would have loved this,' said Lyn, eyeing Eve, a strange smile on her face. 'Did he speak to you?'

Eve frowned.

'Jeff? Of course he did.'

'No. Stan. In the house. Did he speak to you just now? I noticed you didn't come out into the garden with us.'

Eve stared at the woman, her jaw slowly dropping as the smile on Lyn's face grew.

'How did you—'

'I know you think you don't believe, love,' said the medium. 'I know you think I'm a fake,' she whispered so the customers wouldn't hear. 'But sometimes we think things, we believe things, to protect ourselves. Sometimes it can do you good to open your mind and explore the possibility of the thing that scares you being true. What does your gut tell you?'

Eve placed a hand over her gut as the fear swirled around.

'That Stan was trying to tell me something.'

Lyn gave a nod.

'And what does your gut think he was trying to tell you?'

Eve went to answer and then shook her head and shrugged.

'I have no idea.'

'Yes, you do. You have a good idea. What's the first idea that came to you? The message that Stan is trying to tell you. What's the message that you can't stop thinking about?'

Eve looked back to Jeff, now in conversation with Beth as he ate a mince pie. Lyn followed her gaze.

'Your gut is always right, Eve. And there's nothing to be scared of. Stan is happy and at peace. He told me so, in the hallway outside his study, as he watched you and his son talking.'

Lyn patted Eve on the arm and then walked a few steps away before a couple from the tour group approached her, asking excitedly about one of the ghost stories she'd told.

Eve kept her gaze on Jeff and then slowly wandered over.

Beth was laughing at something Jeff had said and she handed Eve a mince pie as she asked him, 'So, have you enjoyed the ghost tour?'

'I have. It's actually quite magical here, isn't it,' said Jeff, looking around the orchard as the brass band ended one song and started another. 'What do you do here for Halloween?'

'We put scary monsters in the trees and last year we did some bat detecting too. If they're around in October, they tend to be attracted to the orchard later at night as the lights attract all the flying insects,' said Eve. 'It's not magical but it's just as much fun. To be honest, I prefer Christmas.'

'I don't know. I like the cider we serve at Halloween,' said Beth. 'I prefer cider to mulled wine.'

'Me too,' Jeff agreed.

'And there's apple bobbing,' Eve added, looking around the orchard, picturing where everything would go. 'And pumpkins. Beth carves them. She's a woman of many talents.'

Beth shrugged.

'I just do what you tell me.'

Jeff smiled at Eve.

'I thought you said most of the ideas were Dad's?'

Eve considered that.

'Well, we use a lot of his ideas. The big spider was his idea. He bought that. You should keep it. I'll leave it here when we pack up.'

Jeff's expression fell.

'Yeah. I still need to talk to my sister about that.' He gave a little shiver and picked up a glass of mulled wine.

'You're cold. Here, take your coat back. I'll run back to the house and get mine.'

'No, no. I'm fine. My coat suits you,' said Jeff, taking the opportunity to look Eve up and down. Eve smiled and, behind Jeff, Beth smirked.

After a moment, Lyn caught Eve's eye before turning back to the group of women she was talking to.

'Oh, I hate to ruin the moment,' Eve said to Jeff and Beth. 'But Lyn basically just told me she's a real medium and that she also spoke to Stan upstairs.'

Jeff stared at her wide-eyed, lowering his hand holding his mulled wine. Beth frowned.

'What do you mean "also spoke to Stan"?' She looked between Jeff and Eve.

'A couple of photos fell off the wall while I was in the study, before I came out here,' Eve explained.

'A couple? I thought it was just the one, of Mum and Dad, with the message.'

'Message?' asked Beth.

'Yeah. "Everything you need is right in front of you". On the back of a picture of Stan with his wife, his arm around her, they both looked so happy. It's a lovely photo.'

'What was the other picture to fall down?' Jeff

asked.

'The one of you,' said Eve and then added quickly, 'and your brother and sister.'

Jeff and Eve stared at each other for a moment.

'I saw Dad in one of the bedrooms,' Jeff told Beth in a quiet voice, his eyes still on Eve. 'He smiled at me, he was happy, and then he looked at Eve.'

Beth raised an eyebrow.

'Sounds to me an awful lot like your dad wanted the two of you to meet. Didn't you say Stan had invited you to Boxing Day dinner this year, Eve?'

Jeff raised an eyebrow.

'Did he?'

Eve blinked rapidly, pulling herself out of Jeff's gaze.

'He does every year,' she murmured. 'I spend Christmas with my parents so I've never been able to make it.' She sighed. 'I wish I had. Just once. I kept meaning to. This year was going to be the year. But then, I never wanted to be the odd one out or intrude. You know, it's a family time.'

'But you were family,' Beth prompted.

'That's what our Boxing Day is,' Jeff agreed. 'Jan comes too, and Harry and Dave who look after the garden. Last year a couple of cousins came with their kids. There were loads of us. It wouldn't have been awkward at all.'

'Oh. Well, now I really regret not going,' said Eve, looking down at her hands, her chest feeling so empty it hurt. How was this possible? To swing from feeling so full of emotion to so empty that the pain was almost too much.

'Don't be silly,' said Jeff. 'We all have our Christmas traditions and you spend yours with your parents. Dad should have invited them too if he really wanted you to come.'

'True,' said Eve, picturing it with a smile. 'That would have been nice. That didn't even cross my mind.'

Jeff took another glass of mulled wine.

'See, you're cold,' Eve pointed out as he cupped his hands around the warm glass. 'Here, take your coat and I'll go get mine.' She took his coat off her shoulders before he could argue. Beth handed her a glass of mulled wine to keep her warm on the walk over and while she was about it, Eve took a gingerbread ghost as well. The piles of treats were getting smaller by the minute and she wasn't going to be the one to miss out.

'At least let me come with you, then,' said Jeff, reluctantly taking his coat and then realising both of Eve's hands were full so he couldn't hand it back. He hesitated, as if about to drape it back across her shoulders but Eve moved too fast.

'Okay. Just in case something jumps out at me.' She flashed him a grin and bit off the tail of the gingerbread ghost. Beth smiled to herself, watching Jeff and Eve walk out of the orchard and away from the lights, chatter and music.

10

The house was dark, other than the sparkling lights of the Christmas tree, and full of echoes as Eve opened the front door and made her way to the coat room. Jeff followed closely, giving another shiver.

'I know the heating's on but we really should get the fire going.'

'The tour group will start going home soon,' Eve explained, pulling her coat on. 'I'll help Beth tidy up out there. You can get the fire going then. Do you want me to take the tour decorations down tonight? I should really, as tomorrow is Christmas Eve.'

'What? Oh no,' said Jeff. 'You can't do it tonight, it's too late.'

'It's still quite early. There'll be plenty of time. Unless you'd like to get settled, in which case I'm happy to come back tomorrow morning. I just thought you might want all of the cobwebs and things taken down before Christmas Eve.' Eve looked up at the large tree thoughtfully, although from the corner of her eye she could see Jeff staring at her.

'Okay,' he said carefully. 'I'll help you take them down tonight. It won't take long. And then you should stay. You've worked so hard today. Sit by the fire and have dinner with me and Jan. Beth can stay too. It'll be nice.'

Eve smiled.

'That does sound lovely. Thank you. If you're sure.'

'Of course,' said Jeff with a nod. 'Absolutely.'

'What are your Christmas plans?' Eve asked. 'What will you do?'

Jeff sighed, looking around the room.

'I think we'll still have it here. Wendy will bring her family and I think Glen's got his son this year. He better do, everything considered. Wendy usually cooks because she enjoys it for some reason and her roast potatoes are to die for. And then Boxing Day.' He glanced at Eve. 'Dad's invitation still stands. You're more than welcome to join us.'

Eve nodded.

'Thank you. I'll do that, if that's okay. Better late than never, right?'

Jeff gave a sad smile.

'Your parents can come too.'

'No. No, they'll understand. I should have come to Boxing Day here a long time ago. Will it just be you and Wendy and Glen though?'

'And Wendy's husband, that'll be awkward, they're not on the best terms right now, so you can save me from that.'

The corner of Eve's mouth lifted up as she watched Jeff think.

'And their children, of course,' he continued. 'Glen and his son. Jan'll be there and Harry and Dave. We've invited the cousins but I'm not sure if they'll come. I think we'll invite some of Dad's friends from the town. It might turn into a little night of remembering Dad.'

'Then I'm definitely coming,' said Eve, giving him what she hoped was a comforting smile. 'You hear that, Stan? I'll be here for Boxing Day,' she called into the house. 'And I hope you'll forgive me for all the times I didn't make it.'

There came no response, which Eve was glad of. She wasn't sure what she'd have done if a light had flickered or another picture had fallen or if they'd heard a voice.

They both jumped as excited gasps and cheers came from outside and both Jeff and Eve turned to the front door.

'What's going on?' Jeff walked to the door and peered out before laughing. Eve followed closely and then gave an excited squeal, pushing past Jeff onto the porch, lit up by fairy lights, to hold out her hand and catch the falling snowflakes.

'It's snowing!' she cried and there were cheers from the orchard in response. Eve laughed, stepping out among the flakes and twirling in her coat. Jeff watched from the porch, grinning. Eve wrapped her coat about her tighter and stepped back into the glow of the porch to watch the snow fall.

'Do you think people will have trouble leaving?' she asked after a moment.

'I doubt it. It's not falling that hard. Not yet,' Jeff said quietly.

'I guess I might have trouble leaving,' Eve murmured, before adding, 'Don't want to get snowed in.'

'Don't you?'

Eve glanced at Jeff to find him just behind her shoulder, gazing at her with soft eyes.

'Look up,' he murmured in her ear.

Her eyes flicked to above their heads and the sprig of mistletoe hanging there. She smiled at Stan's favourite Christmas touch. Then her gaze fell back down to Jeff as he moved closer to her. Her heart racing, she turned to face him, lifting her chin to him, wondering for a moment what to do with her hands.

His lips touched hers in a kiss. He was so warm and his lips so soft. In the background, the brass band began to play We Wish You A Merry Christmas. The tour was finished, the group would be filing back to the front of the house soon. They'd be caught kissing under the mistletoe. Eve considered pulling away but Jeff's hand snaked around her waist, pulling her closer. His lips tasted of the mulled wine and his cologne found its way up her nose. In that moment, she wanted nothing more than to snuggle into his arms and hold him close. The kiss broke but they didn't move apart. Instead, Jeff touched the tip of her nose with his and then pressed his forehead into hers, smiling.

'You know, when you said Dad's message was "everything you need is right in front of you", my second thought was the house. I want to live here properly, make it my home, leave London behind.'

'What was your first thought?' Eve asked breathlessly, looking up into his eyes, the blue twinkling in the low light.

'You,' he said, leaning down and kissing her again. Eve reached up and wrapped her arms around his neck, holding him close. She went up on tiptoe to get closer and he smiled into the kiss.

They broke apart to the sound of applause and found the entire tour group standing on the driveway before them. Squinting in sudden light, both Eve and Jeff looked behind them into the house. The lights had come on, not only in the hallway but in the rooms coming off the hallway.

'Did you do that?' Beth asked Janine, standing to the side of the group close to the porch.

'Not me,' came Janine's voice.

'I think Dad did it,' Jeff murmured, pulling Eve close and wrapping his arms around her in a hug. She did the same, putting her arms around him and resting her head on his chest, breathing in his scent.

From the front of the tour group, Lyn clapped

her hands once with glee.

'Come on then!' shouted Beth. 'It's still snowing out here and it's freezing. Stop canoodling and get out of the way.'

Grinning, Jeff led Eve into the house and turned off the main lights, letting the fairy lights of the Christmas tree and around the porch light the way of the others. He kept an arm around Eve, as if she was planning on going anywhere else. She looked up at him until she caught his eye.

'Wanna stay for dinner, Beth?' Jeff asked, his gaze lingering on Eve.

'You sure you two don't want to be alone?' Beth asked.

'Plenty of time for that,' Eve murmured.

Jeff grinned as Beth playfully threw a gingerbread ghost at Eve.

That's It In A Nutcracker

JENNIFER NICE

1

Beth's teeth ached by the time she pulled the car to a stop. Pulling up the handbrake, she took a deep breath, released her jaw muscles and centred herself. This was the part she hated. Every bump in the road had been agony, every turning had been with bated breath. Beth geared herself up and stepped out of her car, slamming the door behind her. Tentatively, she opened the boot and took away the cardboard walls she'd erected, along with the polystyrene padding and bubble wrap. Gradually, the tiers of the white wedding cake were revealed and Beth sighed in relief at the sight of them safe and sound. Leaving the cake where it was and locking her car, Beth went in search of the wedding planner. Through the grand entrance of the hotel, decorated beautifully with ivy and holly, and straight up to reception. They found the wedding planner who introduced himself as Simon and then helped Beth carry the cake tiers, stand and props into the main reception room.

'There's something wonderful about a Christmas wedding,' said Beth as she started putting the cake together. Simon stood over her, hands on his hips, eyes distant.

'Yeah.'

Beth glanced up at him.

'Everything okay?'

The wedding planner blinked and looked down to Beth.

'Yes, yeah. Sorry. This one's been a bit stressful.' He sighed. 'They're all stressful but the Christmas ones more so.' His eyes grew distant again. 'I never used to find them this bad.'

Beth waited but when he didn't continue, she turned back to the cake. The tiers were in place and she carefully added the white roses, a cascade of iced snow and a dusting of edible gold. Simon focused and grinned.

'That's beautiful.'

'Thank you.' Beth reached into her box of tricks and pulled out a business card that had been languishing there since she'd ordered them. The pile was getting low but it wasn't quite time to order more yet. 'Do you want my card? In case you have any other weddings down this way in the future? Flour Power Bakery. I'm on the high street.'

Simon took the card with some reluctance.

'Thanks but, to be honest, this might be my last wedding.'

'Oh? How come?'

'Sort of sick of organising weddings for other people,' Simon mumbled.

Beth did a double take at him.

'I get that,' she murmured. 'Always the baker, never the bride.' She gave a shrug. 'My friend's an event planner, if you ever want to hand anything over to someone else. I'd be happy to put you in touch. She's been talking about organising weddings. Keeps asking me to go into business with her.'

The wedding planner gave Beth a look.

'Why haven't you agreed?'

Beth gave the cake a final flourish and stepped back.

'Because I know how stressful wedding planning can be. You're not the first wedding planner I've met.'

Simon laughed and then checked the time.

'Speaking of which,' he murmured.

'Are you local?'

'No, I'm based in London. But the bride is from around here and this is a lovely venue.'

Beth nodded.

'If you fancy coming back out this way, my friend is organising a Christmas fair and baking competition this year. She used to do tours up at the Manor – that big house on the hill? – but the owner passed away a year ago. So no more tours, but the bakery competition and fair entry is for charity. Everyone's welcome. If you want to meet her or just fancy taking some time out shopping, getting in the

Christmas mood, you should come along.'

'Are you entering the competition?'

Beth smiled.

'No, I can't. I've been asked to judge, but I'll have a stall so there'll be some of my stuff available. It's all for a good cause. All the proceeds, and I mean nearly every penny as none of us are getting paid for it and we're getting the venue for free, so everything's going to a homeless charity. The old man who used to own the Manor left it to his youngest son, it's a charity close to his heart.'

Simon raised an impressed eyebrow.

'How did your friend get the venue for free? Out of the goodness of his heart?'

Beth barked a laugh and crossed her arms, giving the cake one last going over with her sharp eyes.

'You could say that. They got together last Christmas and they're both smitten. She moved in a few months ago. He couldn't say no to her running an event from their home at Christmas and she couldn't say no to his choice of charity.'

Simon gave a deep sigh.

'Lucky them.'

Beth's smile faded.

'Yeah.'

A silence fell over them until the wedding planner's phone beeped.

'That's the bride. I best go. Thank you so much for the cake, it's beautiful. And maybe I will check out this charity event of your friend's. If nothing else, it's a trip out of the city.'

Beth gave him a smile.

'I hope the wedding goes well.'

'Me too,' said Simon with a laugh before turning away and almost running out of the room. Beth made her exit at a slower amble, enjoying the twinkling fairy lights decorating the room and the tall Christmas tree in the corner. Wandering through the bar, she became distracted by the soft Christmas carols playing over the chatter as she weaved through the wedding guests arriving. Turning into reception, she gave a gentle oof and looked up into familiar brown eyes.

'Sorry,' she said automatically.

He took a second longer, recognition lighting up his features as he smiled and then apologised.

'I didn't know you knew the bride or groom?' Glen Hargreaves asked, his gaze flitting over Beth in her floury jeans and baseball cap, her coat covering the mess beneath. He frowned and met her eyes again.

'Oh yes, I come to every wedding like this. I never want to upstage the bride,' said Beth with a grin, holding out her arms to give him a better view of her outfit. As his frown deepened, she gave a chuckle. 'I'm just delivering the wedding cake,' she explained.

Glen's frown vanished, replaced with a smile.

'Oh, of course. Wonderful. I can't wait to taste it.'

There was a tantalising moment as they stared at one another, Beth frantically trying to work out what a normal person in a normal situation would say next.

'Are you friends with the bride or groom?'

'The groom, strangely,' said Glen, glancing behind her into the bar.

'Strangely?' asked Beth. 'How strange?'

Glen's eyes met hers again and this time they softened. Something shifted inside Beth.

'I worked with him once in London but she's the one from round here, although we hadn't met before. Small world, huh?'

'Yeah. Small world.' Beth caught herself looking at his lips and ripped her gaze back to his eyes. She opened her mouth to say more when a slender arm snaked its way around Glen's arm. It belonged to a tall, equally slender woman with long brown hair so thick that it belonged in a shampoo advert. She was wearing a low cut blue dress that brought out her eyes and Beth became acutely aware that she was wearing a baseball cap at a wedding.

Glen looked down at the woman and gave a small smile. There was a pause as the women looked at one another and then questioningly up at him.

'Beth, this is Joy. Joy, this is Beth. She's the wedding cake baker and friends with Eve.'

'Eve?' asked Joy, holding out her hand for Beth to take.

'Jeff's girlfriend. My brother?'

Joy gave an elegant singular nod and turned back to Beth.

'Pleasure to meet you.'

'And you,' said Beth with a dry mouth. She dropped Joy's limp hand. 'Well, I best be going. Can't be bringing down the wedding party looking like this. Have fun.' Without looking back she scrambled around Glen and Joy, heading for the door.

'Wait.'

Beth stopped but didn't turn back immediately. First, she scrunched her eyes closed as every fibre in her body told her to run as fast as she could for her car. Slowly, she pivoted on her trainer heel to look back up into Glen's eyes.

'Fancy a drink?'

Beth glanced to Joy who was checking her reflection in a mirror on the reception wall.

'Oh, thank you, but I don't want to interrupt or interfere or anything.' Beth stepped back, closer to the door.

'No, no, you won't be. Joy, your friend's here, isn't she?'

Joy nodded.

'Over in the corner.' She waved to someone Beth couldn't see. 'If you don't mind?'

'Of course not,' said Glen, turning back to Beth. 'So, let me buy you a drink. Just one. We've got time before the ceremony starts.'

Beth looked down at herself. She used to dress up for delivering wedding cakes and each time she'd drop off the cake and make it back to her car without seeing anyone but the venue staff and perhaps a wedding planner or one family member making themselves useful. It had been a waste of makeup and fancy dresses. It was never part of the plan to bump into someone she knew on her way out and be asked to stay for a drink.

'Sure. Okay. A small one. And I'm driving so no alcohol.'

A grin broke out across Glen's face.

'Of course. C'mon.' He led the way to the bar and after a moment Beth followed, dragging her trainers into the room filled with dressed up wedding guests.

2

Sitting at the small table Glen pointed out, Beth watched him go to the bar and order their drinks. He smiled at the barman, his eyes bright, teeth flashing. He had a good smile. It didn't seem fair to bump into him at a time like this. His short, dark greying hair was styled, his black suit was impeccable, he looked like he'd lost weight from his gut but maybe that was the magic of being dressed for a wedding. Beth pulled off her baseball cap, permanently dusted with flour and icing sugar, with a large stain of food colouring, and placed it on her lap under the table. She crossed her legs, squeezing her ankles together in an attempt to make herself smaller.

Glen approached, placing a small glass filled with ice and lemonade in front of her and a pint of something golden for himself. She waited until he was settled, his eyes grazing over her sending a familiar sensation through her stomach. Beth glanced back to find Joy still talking to her friend.

'Joy seems nice,' she said.

Glen followed her gaze, holding his pint to his lips.

'She is.' There was a pause as Glen sipped his drink. 'That feels a little out of place,' he said, gesturing with his eyes to a brightly lit-up red and black Nutcracker on the wall. 'Do you think they forgot to take it down?'

Beth swivelled in her chair to look at it.

'Oh, I don't know. Some people find the Nutcracker romantic.'

'Romantic? It's creepy as hell,' said Glen. Beth laughed to herself, turning back to find Glen watching her. 'You like it?' he asked.

She shrugged.

'Actually, yeah. I've always quite liked the Nutcracker.'

Glen smiled to himself, his gaze intense as he looked over her.

'How have you been?' he asked.

'I'm all right. Busy. How about you?'

'Good. It's been a while, hasn't it. I almost didn't recognise you.'

Beth smiled.

'Well, last time we met I was wearing a proper dress and everything.'

'Yeah.'

Beth looked up into the brown of Glen's eyes. His voice was deep, to match his broad chest, and that one word vibrated through the table to her.

'True. I haven't seen Beth the Baker, have I.' Glen grinned again. The last time they'd met, the first time they'd met, he hadn't been smiling much.

'You would have done if you'd come into the café,' Beth pointed out, taking a gulp of her drink. The sooner she was finished, the sooner she could leave, and while a part of her wanted to stay in Glen's presence, the room was getting louder and busier with wedding guests.

Glen shifted, his smile falling.

'I'm sorry I didn't. I meant to. I was going to pop in to get something for the road but we ended up leaving late. I can't remember why.' He frowned. 'The whole trip is a bit hazy.'

Beth's heart pounded.

'Oh? The whole trip?'

Glen met her eyes and for a moment it was just the two of them. Beth blinked herself back into the room.

'Well, not the whole trip.' Glen softened and Beth swallowed hard. 'Do you remember the morning after?'

Beth smiled.

'Not really. I get your point.'

'I remember Boxing Day,' said Glen. 'Really well. It was poignant. I don't think I'll ever forget it. The first Boxing Day after my dad died. It was just like it always was but with this huge hole, this big thing missing.'

Beth ran her finger through the condensation on

her glass.

'I wasn't supposed to be there. Your dad had invited Eve every year and she had never managed to go, but he never invited me.'

'You were being a good friend,' Glen told her. 'Moral support, weren't you?'

Beth smiled.

'Eve was so nervous. She said the first time she met you, you were quite scary. Arguing with Jeff, being every inch the big brother.' She glanced up at the greying broad man in front of her as he stared down at the table in thought. He'd never for a moment seemed scary to her. 'I'm glad I was there for her,' she added gently.

Slowly, Glen lifted his eyes to hers and gave the smallest hint of a smile. Beth inwardly cursed herself. When he'd failed to show up at her café the following day, she'd ordered herself to stop thinking about him. To stop thinking about what had been and what might have been. It had been one evening and it had obviously meant more to her than to him.

'Me too,' he said softly. 'You brought those cookies?'

Beth shrugged.

'Who knows. I bake so much all the time. I'm sure I did bring cookies, it sounds like me.'

'I remember how they tasted. I really should have bought some for the road. I really should have stopped by. I regretted it, you know, the moment I left the town, when I hit the motorway. Even more so when I got home.'

Lacking anything to add, Beth shrugged again.

'If you hadn't been there, I would have been stuck having the same conversations I have every Boxing Day,' Glen added, his gaze back in his pint. 'With Dad's gardeners or with Wendy. It's not Boxing Day if I'm not arguing with my sister in the kitchen. And I just...couldn't. You know? Not last year. Maybe this year.' He looked up and smiled. 'Will you be there this year?'

'Maybe,' said Beth. 'Eve and Jeff haven't said anything yet.'

'They're still going strong?'

It was Beth's turn to smile down into her glass before she took another gulp.

'I've never seen Eve so happy in a relationship.'

When she looked up, Glen had a faint smile lingering on his lips.

'No. Felt a bit destined, didn't it.'

'Very,' Beth agreed.

'Do you believe in that? In destiny?'

Beth blinked, furiously working out how to answer such a question.

'I reckon so.'

'You do. You told me you do.'

'Did I?'

'On Boxing Day. You moved to London as a graduate and got a job in investment banking, of all things. To work off the stress, you would bake and soon people in your office were putting in orders. And you ended up crying one morning, sitting on your kitchen floor, because you realised you wanted to stay home and bake cakes instead of go into the office. But you got up, got dressed, dragged yourself in only to find your senior manager waiting for you with an order for a big wedding cake, and the cheque he gave you made you quit your job.'

Beth stared wide-eyed at the man sitting opposite her.

'You remember all that?'

Colour flushed Glen's cheeks and he looked away.

'It got me thinking,' was all he said.

Beth raised an eyebrow.

'Thinking of quitting your city job and becoming a baker?'

Glen laughed.

'I considered it. Not baking, though. Carpentry. I always wanted to do something with my hands but that was always more Jeff's thing.'

'You should do it,' Beth told him.

He met her eyes for one dazzling moment.

'What could a management accountant of thirty years do with his hands? I tried carpentry. Went on a course and everything. I made a bird house and it was awful. I could have killed birds with it.'

'So, not carpentry then?'

Glen laughed.

'I went back into my office the next day filled

with a new appreciation for my job. I think what I actually needed was a holiday. A breath of fresh air. That's what... That's what Boxing Day was.'

Beth studied him.

'A grief-stricken breath of fresh air?'

Glen's eyes hardened, his features turning serious.

'Maybe it was seeing Jeff moving on so quickly. Maybe it was meeting you.' His lips twitched. 'God knows I needed that kiss.'

Heat ran up Beth's body and she subconsciously tugged at her collar, aware of how red her neck and cheeks must be.

'Glad I could help,' she murmured. When she glanced back, she caught Glen studying her with a roguish smile. Her breath caught. He'd only smiled once or twice when they'd first met so she hadn't been able to dwell on it. She'd thought his smile charming but that didn't quite cover it. It was as if he was planning something beneath it all, as if he knew what he was doing to her. Then the smile would fall away and there were no plans, no knowledge, just her fluttering heartbeat.

'I wish I could remember why I didn't come visit you the next day,' he murmured.

Beth shook herself.

'Well, it's all in the past now. A whole year has nearly passed. And you have Joy and I have cakes to make. People think the summer wedding season is busy but Christmas can be a nightmare. There's mince pies and gingerbread and cookies and fruit cakes that need icing, as well as the usual café stock and Christmas wedding cakes. And now Eve's got me judging her charity baking competition—'

'Oh, yes, I heard about that,' Glen interrupted. Beth used it as an excuse to finish her drink. 'Have to admit, I'm glad she's not doing a ghost tour so close to Christmas. And that she's not holding them regularly anymore. Gave me the creeps. Especially just after Dad passed away. It seemed almost disrespectful. I know, I know.' Glen held up his hands as Beth went to protest. 'He would have loved it. He loved those tours. I know. And I know about the one this weekend. But that's different. It's for Dad, in his memory, which is nice in a way. Still, a charity bake sale, or whatever, feels more correct given the situation.'

'Correct?' Beth cocked her head to the side.

'Yeah. You know, when it was built the owners of the Manor would have pretty much owned this whole town. It's nice that Jeff and Eve are going to do a community event that gives back.'

Beth relented. He had a point.

'That's true. Although the money's going to a London homeless charity.'

Glen shrugged.

'It'll become a thing though, won't it. I know my brother and from what I can tell of Eve, they'll make this a regular thing. Before you know it, the church will have a new roof and there'll be a new community centre.'

Beth smiled despite herself.

'That's Eve all over,' she murmured.

'And you'll be there for each one, making the best cookies I've ever eaten.'

Again, their eyes met.

'You're not coming up for the baking competition, then?' she asked. 'It's only a week before Christmas.'

Glen drained the last of his pint.

'Probably not. My son is spending Christmas with his mother this year, so he's spending the week before with me and the schools haven't broken up yet, so I need to stay home.'

'It's a fair, not a cake sale,' said Beth. 'There'll be stalls of local businesses and a brass band and, yes, a cake sale, but it's a baking competition too. And it's on a weekend. The Saturday before Christmas, just after the schools break up.'

Glen stared at her for a moment.

'I guess I really don't have an excuse, then, do I,' he said.

Beth scraped her chair back.

'You don't have to come just because I got rid of your excuses. I'm sure you have better things to be doing with your son. Last minute shopping or other festive things, right? I didn't mean to tell you what you should be doing.' Beth stopped and took a breath. 'I should be going. The wedding's going to start soon and I never stay this long.' She ran her hands down her clothes, gripping her baseball cap in one hand, pulling her car keys from her pocket with the other.

Glen stood up.

'Okay. Well. Thanks for staying for a drink. It was nice to see you again.'

Beth searched his eyes, wondering if there was anything behind those words.

'It was nice to see you again too.' She meant it. Her heart was still pounding, her palms sweating, but her chest tightened with the realisation that she would have to forbid any further thoughts of him once she left. It was the end of last year all over again, wondering why he hadn't visited, wondering if he was thinking of her, wondering if she should ask Jeff for his number, wondering if she was being stupid.

Except that now she knew. She was being stupid. The man had a beautiful girlfriend on his arm, or at least in the corner of the bar, a full life in London and obviously hadn't spared a single thought for her other than for the cookies she'd baked.

'Enjoy the wedding,' she told him. 'And thank you for the drink.'

'Maybe I'll see you later,' he said.

Beth stopped and turned back to him.

'At Boxing Day,' he added.

Struggling for a breath, Beth smiled and nodded.

'Yeah. Maybe. See you.' She didn't turn back again, walking straight out of the bar, out of the hotel and over to her car. There was no pause as she climbed in behind the wheel, no hesitation to look back. She simply started the ignition and drove away, gravel crunching under the tyres as tears pricked her eyes.

3

It took eight days for Beth to finally stop thinking about Glen during the quiet moments, for him to stop entering her mind as she iced Christmas cakes, to push the memory of their one and only kiss away each time she collapsed on the sofa after a long day. Eight days and Beth hadn't thought of Glen once, until she realised that by thinking that, she had thought of him.

Slamming her rolling pin onto the counter, Beth swore out loud.

'Everything all right, boss?' asked Pete from beyond the kitchen where he was cleaning the café's coffee machine.

'Yeah. Everything's fine. Sorry.' Beth leaned on the worktop. She'd been so close. What was this hold this man had over her? They'd met once, spent one evening together, shared one kiss. He wasn't anything special. A divorced father approaching his mid-fifties with greying hair and a growing beer belly, who lived in London. Beth had dusted her hands of London a long time ago, she had no desire to go back there but that's where Glen's career was, that's where his son was. No, Glen Hargreaves had nothing going for him other than that smile of his, and Beth knew better than to trust a smile like that. No good ever came of them.

'We just sold out of cookies. Again.' Pete's voice pushed through Beth, bringing her away from Londoner smiles and back to her kitchen with a bump. 'Are we doing any more batches?'

'Nope. That's it. Kitchen's closed unless they want something savoury,' Beth called back.

Pete made a noise of acknowledgement and went to give the bad news to whichever customer was waiting. Beth sighed, looking down at the icing she'd been rolling out before Glen forced his way into her thoughts. Shaking her head, she picked up her rolling pin and got back to work. She had this cake to finish icing and then some cupcakes to finish for an early morning order the next day. After that, she'd get a chance to go into the café and help Pete clean. She checked the time on the big clock that hung on the wall between two large chrome refrigerators. It was nearly five. What were the chances of getting the early night she so desperately needed?

Beth pulled a face, putting her weight into the rolling pin. She'd make the time. Maybe an evening to herself resting was just what she needed to finally get Glen out of her head.

She'd just laid the icing over the cake when her phone started ringing. It was sitting on the worktop, away from the food, so Beth hit the answer and speakerphone buttons with her little finger and went back to work.

'Hey,' she called, working the icing onto the cake.

'Hey,' came Eve's voice. 'Am I interrupting? I mean, I know I'm always interrupting but are you free to talk?'

'I'm icing a cake, you're on speakerphone but it's just me in here. Pete's up front. You okay?'

'Yup. Just going through the Christmas fair checklist.'

Beth sighed. She hadn't even looked at the to do list Eve had given her.

'Okay.'

'Can I come visit? I can help clean.'

Beth hesitated but she didn't need to consider it for long.

'Yes, please.'

She could hear Eve pulling on a coat as she said goodbye and then the line went dead. Beth smiled. Eve's relationship with Jeff was finally calming down and finding some sort of normality. Who had a honeymoon period that lasted a year? Beth raised an eyebrow to herself but was gracious to admit that she was only jealous. Everyone around them had begun to assume that this was just what Eve and Jeff's relationship would be, but finally she was emerging from the Manor for activities other than work. Finally, there was a hint of desperation at needing her own space. It had been a while since Eve had spent any quality time in Beth's bakery. Every time they'd met, Beth had gone to the Manor to eat her homemade scones in the orangery with tea that Eve had prepared, usually after fighting Janine, Jeff's housekeeper, for kitchen access.

Beth called for Pete who appeared in the doorway, leaning against the wall, looking every inch as tired as she felt.

'Eve's popping round to talk Christmas fair but she said she'd help out with the cleaning.'

Pete's eyes lit up.

'And you want me to create a to do list for her? Got it, boss.'

Beth laughed.

'I'm not sure Eve can handle another to do list. I know I can't. But yes, you can delegate.'

Pete grinned and gave a mock salute.

'We're down to our last three tables and are mostly sold out,' he updated, glancing back at the sound of the café door opening. 'Best get that.' He vanished and Beth returned her full focus to the Christmas cake.

She'd started decorating it when Eve appeared in the doorway.

'Good early evening to you!' she declared, taking off her coat. 'Pete's already told me what I'm cleaning but there's customers still around. Shall I make a start? Oh, that cake looks good.'

Beth held up a hand to stop her.

'Thank you, it's for the shop tomorrow, so put your eyes back in your head.' She looked up at her friend. 'It's fruit cake.'

'Oh, in that case I won't go anywhere near it. No chocolate cake around?' Eve glanced around the kitchen.

'Cupcakes waiting to be iced. You can have one when I'm done but you need to do the cleaning first. Consider it payment. Then we can talk about the fair, yeah?'

Eve agreed but hesitated before leaving the kitchen. Beth glanced up.

'You all right?'

'Yeah,' said Eve. 'Are you?'

Beth prickled. Eve had known her too long but even when they'd first met, she always knew when something was bothering Beth, however deep she tried to push it.

'Yeah. I'm fine. Go on, Pete will look after you.'

The Christmas cake was finished and ready for the café tomorrow, and Beth was icing the last three cupcakes when Eve came in and collapsed on a stool in the corner of the room.

'I swear, I don't know what I did to Pete to make him hate me.'

Beth laughed and handed Eve a chocolate cupcake sparkling with gold edible glitter. Eve held it for a while, admiring it.

'I don't think he hates you, I think he just needs

a pay rise.'

Eve met Beth's eyes.

'Is he getting one?'

Beth shrugged.

'I'm going to offer him one. I reckon what I actually need is a proper assistant but I don't know if he'd be interested. We'll see.'

'So he could take over the baking for the cafe and you could join me in an events business?'

Beth sighed and aimed her piping bag at Eve.

'No. No, no, no,' she told Eve. 'For the millionth time. Oh, I never did tell you, did I. I talked to the wedding planner at that Christmas wedding a week ago.' Eight days ago actually, thought Beth before pushing Glen out of her head again. 'He seemed really fed up, was talking about giving it all up. So I invited him to the fair, to see if he wanted to meet you. I thought he might want to hand the business over, but who hands a business over to a stranger? I don't know. That's probably why I didn't tell you.'

Eve's eyes had widened as Beth talked.

'That would be amazing, to take over an existing business.' She licked some icing off her finger. 'Is he based here?'

Beth shook her head.

'London.' She started tidying up the kitchen. 'You don't need me to start an events business, you know.'

'I do if it's a food events business.'

Beth gave her friend a look.

'Well, make it a non-food events business then. The ghost tours were good and this weekend's event is all sold out.'

Eve shook her head, mouth filled with cupcake.

'Yeah, it's great but Jeff will only let me hold one ghost tour a year at the Manor. It has to be at Christmas and it's in memory of his father. I don't know, it doesn't feel right doing it without Stan, not regularly. I think that's all over now. Once a year feels right, like a little tradition that's come out of all this.' She swallowed her mouthful and studied the cupcake. 'I'll figure it out. I'm enjoying doing project management at the moment, but it can't last forever.'

'You don't like the company you're with?'

Eve shrugged.

'They're too small to progress, I think. Plus, after a while all those charts and things are going to get boring. No, I want to get back to events. Maybe I need to speak to some wedding planners.' Eve refocused on Beth. 'I could recommend you for wedding cakes. Would that be allowed?'

Beth smiled.

'I'd be disappointed if you didn't.'

Eve laughed and finished the cupcake in two big bites.

'So, the fair,' she started.

'You'll never guess who I bumped into at that wedding,' said Beth at the same time. They looked up at one another.

'Who?' asked Eve.

'No, no. You're right. Let's talk about the fair. I'll start baking for it tomorrow.' Beth put her hands on her hips, surveying the kitchen in thought. 'I think I'm suitably ahead now but I would like an early night tonight.'

'Of course.' Eve nodded. 'Who did you bump into?'

Beth bit her lip and then met her friend's eyes.

'Glen.'

Eve blinked.

'Glen Glen? Jeff's big brother Glen?'

Beth nodded slowly as Eve's eyes lit up.

'What happened? Did you find some more mistletoe?'

'No. No, he was a guest at the wedding. We bumped into each other as I was leaving and he was arriving. He was with this gorgeous woman and I...' Beth looked down at herself. 'I looked like this, actually.'

'So you looked gorgeous as well. Continue,' said Eve.

Beth flashed her a smile.

'And nothing. He bought me a drink and we had a chat and then I left. He didn't tell Jeff he was in the area?'

Eve shrugged.

'Jeff did speak to him but he didn't come say hello. Probably in a rush to get back to London.'

'Probably,' Beth murmured.

'Jeff hasn't mentioned that he's seeing someone though. I wonder who the woman was.'

'Well, it doesn't matter. Maybe he'll bring her to Boxing Day. He didn't seem to know if Jeff was doing Boxing Day this year?'

'Of course he is,' said Eve. 'It's tradition. And you're invited, of course. But I get it if you don't want to come,' she added quickly.

'Thanks. I might skip it this year.'

There was a pause as Beth finished tidying and Eve watched her.

'So, you talked about Boxing Day, huh?'

Beth sighed and looked back to Eve.

'We did.'

'And?'

'And nothing. There's really nothing to tell.'

'But he bought you a drink?'

'And we caught up. He was being polite, Eve. That's all.'

'Did you want something more?'

Beth hesitated.

'Maybe,' she said quietly. She mentally shook herself. 'Let's talk about the fair.'

'What was the wedding like?' Eve asked, ignoring her. 'Was it pretty?'

'The sct up was beautiful,' Beth told her. 'But how could it not be? It was all Christmas trees and twinkling lights and flowers. Hard to go wrong with a Christmas wedding. As long as it's tasteful.'

'Hmm.'

Beth looked up at Eve and raised an eyebrow.

'Thinking about a Christmas wedding, are we?'

Eve's cheeks grew pink and she waved Beth away.

'It was just a thought. It would be fitting, wouldn't it.'

'Have you talked about getting married?'

Eve held back a grin and nodded.

'We have. I've dropped hints about a ring. I just don't know how far it'll get me.'

Beth stepped over to Eve and wrapped her arms around her friend in a tight hug.

'You better tell me when he proposes. I want to be in the top five of first people to know,' she whispered into Eve's ear. Eve laughed, hugging her back.

'You'll be the third person to know, straight after my parents.'

Beth gave her another squeeze and then pulled away. They grinned at one another.

'So.' Beth clapped her hands. 'The fair. What did you want to discuss?'

'Oh, you know, what you're bringing, what you need, where things are going, timings.'

'That's everything then,' said Beth.

Eve nodded.

'Yup. Oh, hey, want me to ask Jeff for Glen's number?'

Beth nearly tripped over her own foot as she cleaned the kitchen.

'Absolutely not!'

'Why not? I can ask Jeff about this woman Glen was with. Ask if he's single? I'll definitely check he's coming Boxing Day and who he's bringing.'

'Eve, no.'

'Why would he buy you a drink if he's not interested?'

'If he was interested, he wouldn't have waited a year to buy me a drink,' said Beth, turning off the lights and herding Eve into the café. The floor was sparkling clean, the chairs neatly tucked under each table. Beth scraped back two chairs and gestured for Eve to sit.

'I'm off, Beth. Unless there's anything else?' asked Pete from the corner of the room, pulling on his coat.

'No, you go. Thanks so much.'

Pete grinned and gave them both a strange little bow.

'Good evening, ladies. Don't stay up too late.'

'Night, Pete,' Eve called as Pete vanished through the door and up the street. She turned back to Beth. 'What if Glen has spent the last year thinking about you, unable to get you out of his head, and suddenly there you are. He bumps right into you and finally does the right thing, buys you a drink and then, once again, you slip out of his life.' Eve sighed.

'I think you've been in a happy relationship for too long,' said Beth. 'That's not how life works.'

'It worked for me. I'm mean, not exactly like that, but sort of.'

Beth fetched them bottles of lemonade from the fridge under the counter and sat heavily in her chair.

'We're not all as lucky as you, Eve.'

4

The early night had done wonders and Beth was whistling as she approached her café and bakery on the high street. The wind had picked up but it was an otherwise dry and quite bright December morning. Today was going to be a long one, with yule logs and cakes to bake for the shop along with cookies for the ghost tour that weekend, getting organised for the fair and—

Beth stopped, her momentum forcing her forward one last step. Outside her locked café door was Glen Hargreaves, peering through the glass. She considered turning and running, and she stopped herself from flattening her body against the hairdressers' window next to her as he slowly spun to look up and down the high street. Glen's features brightened when he saw her. She had no choice but to keep walking, albeit slower than before and without any whistling. Heart thumping, she attempted to return his smile as she drew closer. He wasn't wearing a suit this time, but jeans and a jumper covered by a long black coat, topped with a red scarf wrapped around his neck.

'Good morning,' he said. 'I thought it was about time I popped in for those cakes.'

Beth stared at him and then, because she couldn't help it, her smile became genuine.

'You're a bit early. As you can see, we're not open yet.' She gestured to the "closed" sign on the door.

'No. But the hotel I was staying at couldn't do a proper breakfast, something about their oven breaking, and I seem to remember Jeff mentioning that you do a fry up. Even though it's a bakery.' Glen looked up at the shop and then glanced back to her. 'Did I remember that wrong?'

Beth shook her head, pulling out her keys.

'No, we do a full English but you'll have to wait longer than usual. You know, seeing as I'm not even inside yet.'

Glen grinned and followed her into the café.

'I can go away and come back if you like?' he offered, preparing to take off his coat.

'No, it's okay. Take a seat, I'll be right with you.' Beth hurried into the back, turning on the coffee machine as she passed, and took a while to take off her coat. Gradually her heart rate slowed, her breathing returned to normal, and her thoughts began to make more sense.

What was he doing here?

Should she call Eve? She really wanted to call Eve. Had Eve said something to Jeff?

Beth chewed on her lower lip as she tied her hair back and pulled on her apron. What would happen if she called Eve? They'd argue, in hushed tones, and she still wouldn't have the answers she wanted. No, the answers lay in the café. Taking a deep breath, Beth stepped back behind the counter and began making a coffee for herself.

'What would you like?' she asked Glen who had found a table for two in the corner. He'd removed his coat and was unwrapping his scarf as he looked up at her. 'I've got sausages, bacon, hash browns, toast, beans, tomatoes, mushrooms, black pudding, and we have veggie and vegan options too.'

Glen's eyes widened as she talked.

'Erm, yes please?' he said. 'Not veggie or vegan though. I'm a meat eater.'

Beth gave a singular nod.

'Coffee?' she asked.

'Please. Black.'

Beth worked behind the counter in silence, aware of Glen's eyes on her as she took him his coffee. She placed the cup down without spilling a drop.

'I'll go cook the food,' she murmured, flashing him a polite smile.

'Join me?'

Beth stopped and turned back.

'I mean, if you can. Would you like to join me?' Glen looked away, down at the table, his fingers playing with the cup full of coffee. Beth blinked, glancing up at the front door. There was no sign of other customers and while she had a full day to be getting on with, her stomach was already grumbling from her lacking breakfast of an apple.

'You want me to join you for breakfast?' she asked.

Glen nodded.

'So we can talk. If you have the time. If not, I'm happy to follow you around while you work.'

Beth laughed and immediately caught herself, pulling her lips back down. Glen watched her, bemused.

'Okay. Hang on,' Beth relented, disappearing into the kitchen. As she passed, she paused to turn on the soft Christmas music that usually filled the café this time of year, along with the fairy lights that decorated the panelled walls and large window. Glen looked around, surprised, and then chuckled to himself. Beth watched for a moment and then went to turn the oven on.

While cooking their breakfasts, Beth made the decision to keep the "closed" sign on the door. When Pete arrived, she sent him out to buy last minute supplies. He glanced at Glen, raised his eyebrows at her and left with a smirk on his face.

The next time Beth entered the café it was with a full English for Glen and a smaller version for herself. She sat opposite him and took a moment to stop and appreciate the breakfast she hadn't been expecting.

'This looks incredible,' came Glen's voice. She looked up at him and gave a smile.

'No problem. I hope it tastes as good.'

'I'm sure it does.' Glen picked up his knife and fork and started to dig in. Beth went slower, watching Glen as his eyes closed at the taste of the bacon.

'I'm glad you could finally swing by,' said Beth. 'What are you doing here? Another Christmas wedding? And if so, why am I not doing the cake?'

Glen's chewing slowed as he met her eyes. He swallowed and sipped his coffee.

'Well,' he started. 'This weekend is the ghost tour and I thought Jeff might want a hand. Maybe it would be nice to be involved this year, see what all the fuss is about. Especially as it's in memory of Dad.'

Beth nodded, playing with her food.

'How come you're not staying with them?' she asked.

Glen shrugged.

'I didn't want to impose. They're still very lovey-dovey, aren't they? I'm not sure if it's sickening or...'

Beth glanced up.

'Or?'

'Honestly? I get a little jealous, I guess.' Glen shoved a forkful of food into his mouth while Beth considered this.

'What about that woman you're seeing? Are things not lovey-dovey with her?' Beth inwardly flinched. She didn't want to know the answer.

Glen frowned.

'What woman?'

Beth hesitated. No, she had definitely been introduced to a beautiful woman on Glen's arm at the wedding.

'The woman you were with at the wedding?'

After a moment, recognition flooded Glen's eyes.

'Oh. Her.' He loaded up his fork. 'I'm not seeing her. She's a friend who didn't have anyone to go with, I didn't have anyone to go with, so we decided to go together.'

Beth let that settle for a moment, holding back the smile that was desperately forcing itself onto her lips.

'Oh,' she said, covering her mouth with a gulp of coffee.

'To be honest, I was quite happy living the single life until Jeff and Eve got cosy together. I'm happy for them, I really am. It's been a long time since Jeff had something like this. Been a long time since I have too.' Glen drifted off, staring past Beth, absent-mindedly putting his fork into his mouth.

'Do you see them often?' Beth asked, taking steady breaths, trying to calm her heart rate. 'Or have you been feeling this way since Boxing Day when they started all this lovey-dovey stuff?'

Glen came back to the room, focusing on her. The heat rose to her cheeks and she looked down to her food.

'No but I chat with Jeff regularly. You can hear it in his voice and sometimes hear her in the background. And then there're the times when Jeff does a video call.'

Beth pulled a face.

'Oh, he's one of those.'

Glen laughed.

'He is. He does it for work, when he can't get on site, and it's trickled into his personal life. Eve doesn't do video calls? I would have thought if an architect does them then an event planner definitely would.'

'Well, I don't know about professionally, but personally Eve does frantic calls when she needs to talk, immediately, usually here with cake.' Beth smiled. 'I don't mind. She usually ends up helping to clean or something.'

'I can do that,' said Glen, his voice soft. Beth swallowed too hard, glancing up at him.

'You don't have to. She just feels guilty about all the free cake she nabs off me.' Beth shrugged. 'So, you're helping at the ghost tour?'

'I'm going to try. I've been told to do whatever Eve says.'

'Eve knows you're here?'

Glen glanced up.

'Yeah.'

'And you've spoken to her?'

'Of course. I only arrived late last night. I had dinner with them.'

Beth stared at him, wondering how to broach the subject.

'Are you okay?' he asked.

'Mmm, yup. Yeah. I'm fine.' Beth concentrated on her food. She couldn't just ask the question out right, that would be the perfect way of telling Glen just how much he'd gotten under her skin without Eve necessarily having said a word. No. The only option here was to ride it out. Or change the subject.

She looked back up at him.

'And then you're back off to London?'

'Yeah. Back to work for the last week before Christmas. Kind of wish I could take that week off, seems silly to go back just for five days. A lesson for next year, perhaps. I forgot how much I miss this place, and the Manor. Jeff hasn't changed much yet. I'm hoping he doesn't change it too much. Just the carpets, maybe.' Glen chewed thoughtfully. 'Do you think Eve will change a lot?'

Beth smiled.

'You've got nothing to worry about. Eve loves that house just as much as Jeff does.'

Glen nodded.

'They're sickeningly perfect for each other, aren't they,' he said.

Beth laughed.

'Yup.'

There was a pause as Beth concentrated on finishing her breakfast, acutely aware that Glen was watching her.

'Are you seeing anyone?'

Beth narrowly missed a piece of toast going down the wrong way but was forced to cough anyway. That bemused look twitched at Glen's mouth again before it turned into something that was irritatingly devilish. It suited him more than she cared to admit. She managed to chew her mouthful and swallow properly, centring herself as she did.

'No,' she said eventually. 'I'm not. I'm guessing you're not either if you're taking friends to weddings?'

Glen smiled.

'No. I'm not seeing anyone. I haven't had a serious relationship for a long time. They never seem to end well, do they? That's probably why I went to the wedding with Joy. Casual relationships seem just about do-able.'

Beth swallowed.

'Casual?'

'Yeah. Less chance of getting hurt.'

'I absolutely disagree.'

Glen met her eyes.

'How's your son?' Beth mopped up the last of her breakfast.

'He's good. Doing his exams in the summer, already thinking about university. I'm not sure what I'll do without him trashing my house every other week.'

Beth relented, giving a soft smile. Still, she couldn't help herself.

'He's not the reason you're avoiding a serious relationship, then? He's a young adult now, almost the right age for getting his own heart broken.'

Glen frowned.

'Even more reason to protect him.'

Beth gave him a curious look.

'Heartbreak is a rite of passage,' she told him. 'And isn't it worth the risk? If you can get the kind of love that Jeff and Eve have?'

Glen didn't respond. He watched her as she tidied their plates away, and remained silent, finishing his coffee, as she opened the café and positioned herself behind the till as customers started popping in.

5

The sky was heavy with thick, iron grey cloud as Beth turned off the country road and her car trundled up the long driveway to the Manor house. The trees that lined the driveway were already decorated with fairy lights. Finding a space next to a small, sleek, black BMW, Beth stopped and stared at the car beside her. It was Glen's. She narrowed her eyes. Or was it his sister's? No, no, it was Glen's. Wendy wasn't here this weekend, or at least neither Glen nor Eve had mentioned her.

Taking a deep breath, Beth stepped out of her car, slammed the door and then jumped, her stomach constricting, her heart leaping painfully. Hand on her chest, breathing hard, Beth cursed Eve and all she stood for. In front of her, at the entrance to the orchard, was a robed figure with long, clawed fingers protruding from over-sized sleeves. Beth stared at it for a moment but it didn't move and, after a moment's recovery, her stomach seemed to agree that it wasn't real.

'Beth!'

'What in the name of Christmas is that, Eve?' Beth turned on her friend as Eve skipped out of the Manor's porch towards her. Eve stopped and followed Beth's pointing finger. She laughed which only stirred the anger in Beth's belly.

'It's a gift from Jeff. Did it scare you?'

'I need new underwear,' Beth told her, joining Eve at the back of her car and opening the boot. Eve cackled.

'That can be arranged,' she said, staring down with glee as Beth revealed trays of shortbread ghost biscuits and some strangely shaped gingerbread cookies. 'Is that... Are those... You've made Scrooge cookies?'

Beth glanced up at the fake hooded figure beckoning them to the orchard.

'Give that thing an oil lamp and maybe they're him,' she mumbled.

'Oh, Beth, I love them. You're so clever.'

Beth smiled, settling back. She'd put more work into those Scrooge cookies then she cared to admit. She bent to pick up a tray and Eve did the same.

'How's it going?' Beth asked as she followed Eve into the house. The foyer was decorated as it always was for these things, with beautiful Christmas lights and the odd fake spider web in the corner. This year's tree stood by the staircase, filling the space and sending Christmassy shadows up the walls. Up the stairs, tweaking the angel placed on top, was Jeff. Beth hesitated but only for a moment. She'd walked in once, carrying a tray of cookies, to find Jeff's father standing on the exact same step, placing the angel carefully on the top of the tree. Jeff was almost the spitting image of Stanley Hargreaves and for a moment there, Beth could have sworn she saw a ghost.

Jeff grinned down at her.

'Hey, Beth. You all right?'

'All good, and you?'

Jeff nodded, happy with the angel, and made his way down the stairs to join them.

'Look at these Scrooge cookies, for crying out loud,' Eve told him, brandishing her tray. 'She's out done herself this year.'

'Amazing,' said Jeff, leaning around the tray of cookies to kiss Eve's lips.

'Thanks,' said Beth, wondering how Eve got a kiss for simply pointing them out when she'd been the one to do all the hard work. Not that she wanted a kiss from Jeff. Of course, that was the moment that Glen decided to walk around the corner and straight into Eve. He skidded to a stop and held up his hands.

'Sorry.' He skirted around her, his eye catching Beth's.

'Look at these Scrooge cookies, Glen. Isn't Beth clever?' Eve showed Glen the contents of her tray.

'Very,' said Glen.

It was skirting on the borders of patronising

now. Beth pulled a face.

'Clever and heavy,' she said pointedly to Eve, nudging her slightly in the direction of the kitchen.

'Oh, boys, there's another two trays in Beth's car. Can you grab them?'

'Sure.' Jeff led Glen out of the house and Beth followed Eve to the kitchen where they placed the trays on the wide, wooden worktops. Janine was cleaning by the sink and a teenage boy with dark hair and Glen's mouth was sitting at the kitchen table, staring down at his phone.

'Good evening, Beth. Is it evening yet?' asked Janine.

'Hey, Jan. Just about. Right, what can I help with?' Beth asked, looking around. 'Are these all going out in the orchard as usual?'

'Yup,' said Eve. 'I just need to dig out the trestle tables. Rob can help, can't you, Rob?'

Eve and Janine both turned to the boy at the table but he was too engrossed in his phone to notice. 'Rob?' Eve repeated, knocking on the table.

He looked up.

'You can help with the trestle tables? Yeah?'

'Sure,' said Rob glumly.

Beth caught Eve's eye.

'Rob, you remember Beth from last year's Boxing Day, right? She's the baker. Look at these Scrooge cookies.'

Beth sighed and waited to see if Glen's son would grace her by looking up in her general direction. He didn't.

'Yeah, hi,' he muttered.

'Hi,' Beth murmured. She turned back to Eve. 'Right, I'll help set up but then I think I need to go.'

'What? Why?'

'You have extra help this year with Glen and Rob. You don't need me.'

Eve searched Beth's eyes while Beth blinked, unsure of how much she wanted her friend to work out.

'Set up in the orchard and see how you feel?' Eve offered.

'Fine, maybe I can get your new orchard guardian to help out too.'

Eve grinned and patted Beth on the arm.

Rob might have been quiet but he pulled his weight, helping Beth set up two trestle tables in the orchard. Beth couldn't help but keep her eye on the fake robed figure at the entrance. Turning her back on him seemed to go against her instincts.

'What do you think of that?' she asked Rob, nodding to the figure. He paused in laying out the ghost biscuits to study the robed statue.

'Pretty good,' he said. 'Made me jump when I first saw it.'

'Yeah, me too. Kinda sweet of Jeff to buy it for Eve when he originally said no more ghost tours here.'

'They are a bit tacky,' said Rob, stepping back to consider his work before moving a biscuit ever so slightly to align it with the others. Beth watched him.

'I didn't know you were here with your dad,' she said, arranging the Scrooge cookies to match his display.

'I only came up this morning,' said Rob. 'Mum dropped me off. Dad said I should come enjoy the tour.' He rolled his eyes.

'But ghost tours are tacky,' said Beth.

'Christmas is worse,' said Rob.

Beth watched him for a moment.

'Why do you say that?'

Rob shrugged.

'Mum and Dad don't really talk. You think it means you get two Christmases and more presents but actually you just get the same but in two different places. And if you're lucky, they won't argue when they swap you. Mum married Steve last year and now she's pregnant.'

'I'm sorry. That must be hard.'

Rob shrugged.

'I'm leaving home soon, so what do I care.'

Something twisted in Beth's stomach. This was why Glen didn't want a serious relationship. It was as if all the blocks suddenly fell into place to form a picture of Rob.

'What are you going to do when you leave home?'

Again, Rob shrugged.

'Study, get a good job. Only see them at the holidays.'

'That sounds lonely.'

Rob looked up at Beth.

'What did you do?'

'I studied, got a good job, made sure I saw my family at the holidays.'

'And it was lonely?'

Beth nodded.

'And exhausting. If you do that, if you keep running around trying to earn money and build a career and keep forgetting to replenish all that energy and soul destroying muck with things that you love and that fill you with joy, soon you'll be an empty cask unable to get out of bed. Or out of the fridge, in my case. I certainly couldn't make it to the door. Do yourself a favour and skip that bit. Find a job you can enjoy and fill the gaps in your life with things and people you love. And, if you can, include your family in that. They love you.'

Rob turned back to the biscuits and cookies.

'These are good,' he said.

'Thanks. Please don't say you love the Scrooges. Eve's already said it enough for everyone.'

That earned a smile.

'They're all right. I like these.' Rob pointed to the biscuits that Jeff and Glen had brought in from her car. 'The soldiers.'

'The Nutcracker,' Beth told him. 'They're my favourite too.'

'Yeah, I had a toy one when I was little. Dad hated it.' Rob smiled to himself. 'I've still got it somewhere but I keep it at Mum's. Out of respect for Dad.'

'Well, it's not just you and me who like him. They're a bestseller in my bakery,' Beth told him.

'What's it like? Running your own business?'

Beth smiled at Rob.

'It fills me with joy.'

'That's not really an answer, is it.'

Beth laughed.

'No, it's not. Honestly? It's really hard work. You know I said I didn't get to see a lot of the people I loved before? Well, starting this business, I still didn't get to see people. Not until recently. I still had to force myself to make the time. But after a few years, when the business was established and I could afford to hire some help, everything just fell into place. But then, I'm a baker, I tend to get invited out a lot if I bring cookies and cake. Case in point.' Beth gestured to the orchard. Eve or Jeff had hung a creepy ghost in one of the apple trees and everywhere was lit by twinkling Christmas lights. The tour would end here with a brass band playing while the guests ate the biscuits and drank mulled wine or juice. Janine would appear soon with the mulled wine, if she hadn't delegated the task to Jeff or Glen.

'I don't really know what I want to do yet. Just that I want to be good at it,' said Rob.

'Well, you're good at bakery displays. I love what you've done there. Maybe you're a designer of some sort. Or a baker.' She gave him a nudge and he smiled.

There was a pause as Beth brushed down her hands and did her usual triple check of everything.

'You like my dad, don't you?'

Beth stopped, a chill running over her despite her thick coat and woolly hat. She turned back to Rob.

'Why do you say that?'

'Kinda obvious. You look at him differently to everyone else. He really wanted to stop by the bakery and buy some of your cakes last year. I felt bad about that.'

'Why on earth would you feel bad about it?'

''Cause I'm the reason we didn't,' said Rob. 'I was sick and sort of ordered Dad to take me home. He said he just wanted to stop by but he couldn't. We reckon I ate too much the night before. I was up in the middle of the night being sick.' Rob glanced up at Beth. 'Sorry.'

Beth stared at Rob for a moment as the new blocks of information fell into place.

'Don't be sorry. That wasn't your fault at all. You didn't make yourself sick. Did you?'

Rob pulled a face.

'No.'

'Well then. Just be careful how much you eat tonight,' Beth added quietly. Her heart leapt as Rob laughed.

'Well, I like you,' said Rob. 'And it would be nice

if Dad was happy again. He deserves to be happier.' He looked over the displays he'd helped create and then shoved his hands in his pockets and ambled out of the orchard, side-stepping the robed figure as he went. Beth watched him go. A breeze lifted the ends of her hair as the realisation dawned on her that she was alone in the orchard.

'Wait up! Don't leave me here!' She jogged after Rob, squeezing past the robed figure and holding her breath as if being so close to it would bring it to life.

6

As the guests started arriving, Beth escaped back to the orchard on the pretence of waiting for the band to arrive. Soon after, Jeff and Janine carried the mulled wine, juice and an array of glasses through so Beth helped to arrange them.

'Are you all right here?' Jeff asked.

'I am,' said Beth.

Jeff studied her for a moment.

'You're hiding, aren't you.'

Beth grinned.

'Why yes, yes I am.'

Jeff huffed.

'Bit jealous I didn't think of hiding here. It's a bit chilly, though. Wouldn't you rather come hide in the kitchen?'

'No, I'm okay. I'll help the band set up when they arrive and I'll be here when the guests finish up.' Plus hiding away in the kitchen meant being social with the others and it was nice to just have a moment to herself. Not just to get some time away from Glen and the emotions he evoked but she wasn't entirely keen in that moment to be in the same room as Glen, his brother and his son. Right now she could only handle one Hargreaves at a time.

Janine double-checked that Beth really meant to stay in the orchard and then she and Jeff wandered back to the warm house. As they left, Beth let out a long exhale and relaxed. There was a wonderful silence to the orchard in the darkness. There weren't many lights on in the house, the main one coming from the large kitchen towards the back, almost out of Beth's view. The other main light source was from the Manor's porch where fairy lights spiralled up the columns of wood and reflected off the holly leaves that made up the wreath hanging on the door. The normal light above the front door didn't stand much of a chance. The low light levels meant that above her head, between the drifting cloud, Beth could make out the night sky and winter stars. An icy breeze moved through the trees, finding its way beneath Beth's coat and hat. Shivering, she turned on the outside heaters Jeff had positioned around the tables. While she waited for them to warm up, she rubbed her hands together, pulling out her gloves and slipping them on. Checking that there was no one around, she jogged on the spot for a bit and then considered the unprofessional temptation to eat a ghost biscuit.

Thankfully that was the moment the band

arrived and Beth became caught up in helping them to unpack their instruments and set up in their usual spot. They'd been doing this for a few years now and while Beth hardly saw them throughout the rest of the year, it was a little like seeing old friends. A couple were regulars at her café and she had to smack their hands away from the cookies, grinning at the cheers when she produced a Tupperware box filled with the additional biscuits and cookies she'd made just for them.

They helped themselves to a cup of mulled wine each, with juice for the two drivers, and set up, ready for Lyn, the tour's medium and psychic, to lead the guests down to the orchard. Beth's stomach flipped as Janine, Jeff, Glen and Rob appeared before the guests. Glen and Rob were introduced to the band and everyone found positions at the trestle tables, ready to hand out mulled wine, juice and treats. Beth smiled at Rob as he joined her by the biscuits, checking over his work to see if anything had moved.

'Don't worry, I kept them safe,' she murmured to him.

He gave a small smile.

'You weren't tempted to eat them with no one else here?' he asked.

Beth produced the almost empty Tupperware box and offered him a broken ghost biscuit.

'Always bring extra,' she told him. Rob reached into the box and pulled out half a ghost. 'Take a half

Scrooge too, if you like gingerbread.' Rob did as he was told, shoving the gingerbread into his mouth. His eyes lit up and he made all the right noises as he chewed his first mouthful.

'Anyone else?' Beth asked, offering the box around. Janine took a gingerbread Scrooge while Jeff grabbed some broken bits from the bottom. Glen glanced at her and pulled out a shortbread ghost. The last one.

'If you don't mind?'

'Of course not.' She gave him a big smile but he looked away, taking a bite from the biscuit. Beth's stomach dropped and she turned back to the table, putting the box away. Rob was still working his way through his own biscuit but shot his father a look which Beth was probably not supposed to see.

There came the rumble of chatter and then a small shriek followed by laughter as Lyn led the tour guests past the robed figure and into the orchard. She finished the last of her story and then Eve led the round of applause before the band started up and the guests made their way eagerly to the tables of goodies. Beth allowed herself to be caught up in chatting to people, handing out biscuits and cookies in paper napkins over the din of the brass band. It was enough to make her forget Glen as the whole orchard became filled with the sound and taste of Christmas.

'How did it go?' she asked Eve when she got the chance.

'Really well,' said Eve. 'I don't think I'm going to be able to ever stop doing this, am I? Every year. The Hargreaves Christmas Ghost Tour.'

'Maybe one day run by Mrs Eve Hargreaves.' Beth gave her friend a wink and a ghost biscuit.

Eve laughed, eyes widening on sight of the biscuit. She was out of breath as she took a bite. Beth stepped back and studied her.

'You okay?'

Eve nodded, eyes scanning the orchard. Beth followed her gaze as it landed on Jeff.

'You're worrying about something,' Beth murmured. 'What is it?'

Eve sighed and stepped closer to Beth to whisper, 'I have a feeling Jeff might propose.'

Beth leaned away, looking Eve in the eye.

'On the porch? Under the mistletoe?' Beth's heart pounded.

Eve nodded.

'Why? Just because it would be ridiculously romantic? Or because he's done something to make you think he's planning it?'

Eve shrugged.

'I'm not sure. It just suddenly occurred to me that it would be sort of perfect.'

Beth laughed.

'He's not going to, Eve. Relax. Enjoy your event.'

'Why don't you think he will?'

Beth raised an eyebrow.

'Because you didn't tell him to.'

'He's creative. He has a mind of his own. And it's hard to forget our first kiss anniversary.'

'Is it? Because you seem to have forgotten that your first kiss under the mistletoe on the porch happened the day before Christmas Eve and today is not that day.'

Eve sagged.

'Oh. I had forgotten that. And that's Jeff's fault, making me change the date of this tour.' She sighed heavily. 'Well, there go the butterflies. At least I can relax now.'

'Sorry.' Beth slipped an arm around Eve and squeezed her. Eve threw her arms around Beth and gave her a tight hug.

'It's okay. You've also reminded me why I don't have one of your chocolate yule logs sitting in my cupboard yet.'

Beth laughed.

'I'm making them soon. There'll be one with your name on it.'

Soon Eve was distracted by guests thanking her and saying goodbye. Beth wandered back to the tables to check the supply levels. All of the ghost biscuits were gone and there were only two Scrooges left. Rob had also disappeared, leaving only crumbs behind.

'Do you think people will want those?'

Beth looked up at Jeff as he studied the two gingerbread cookies left, forlorn, on their own.

'I reckon you can have them,' she told him. He

gave her the charming Hargreaves grin and snatched them up.

'Thanks.'

'Hey,' Beth called him back as he turned to make his escape. 'I don't suppose you've talked to Eve about getting married?'

Jeff blinked.

'What?'

'It's just that, if you haven't yet you might want to. You know, talk about it. Or think about it.'

Jeff looked beyond her to where Eve was chatting away. Then he smiled, bit the head off a Scrooge and gave Beth a single nod.

'No worries,' he said around the gingerbread.

Beth caught herself grinning as she watched him take the other Scrooge to Glen. Jeff said something to his brother who looked up to Beth before turning quickly away. Beth watched him curiously.

The evening ended quietly. There were no declarations of love, no kissing under the mistletoe that hung on the porch, no proposals. Only happy customers, a tired but content and slightly sloshed band, and an exhausted team of helpers. Eve thanked everyone, gave Beth a hug and invited her in for a drink. Beth made her excuses. She had chocolate yule logs to make. That was enough for Eve to carry the empty trays back to Beth's car and wave her off. Once home, Beth kicked off her shoes, found a box of broken shortbread ghosts in an old biscuit tin she kept on the worktop, poured herself a glass of wine, and collapsed on the sofa to relax and feel the throbbing of her feet. She needed a holiday. A proper couple of weeks off and away from everything, but that couldn't happen until she'd asked Pete if he wanted a promotion and maybe hired another helper. Still, the idea of Christmas Day and Boxing Day off was just about enough for now. She would sleep all Christmas Day morning and spend the rest of the day with her family. Then, Boxing Day would be spent with... Beth tensed. There he was again, forcing his way into her thoughts. Glen Hargreaves. Who had bought her a drink when he could have let her walk away, who had a wonderful excuse for not coming to see her the year before, who had just pretty much ignored her throughout the whole ghost tour evening. Beth savagely bit through a shortbread ghost. She didn't have the energy to figure him out which, in hindsight, was probably why she'd been single all these years.

7

'So, what I'm proposing,' said Beth as Pete sat back in his chair, trying to hide the way he was nervously rubbing his hands together, 'is promoting you. I haven't figured out a title yet. I thought you could help me with that. Café Manager perhaps. And then I'll hire someone new and they'll report to you in the café, so you can delegate stuff to them. What do you think?' Beth held her breath.

Pete considered this, pursing his lips a little.

'I'd still be working in the café? But I'd be in charge.'

'Yes. You'll be freeing me up to just bake. You'll be taking the café stress off me. I mean, you'll still have to do some of the stuff you do now but you'll have someone to delegate to, more time off because we should be able to stagger shifts, and more pay.'

Pete narrowed his eyes.

'And you can afford that?'

'I can. Just about.'

'I'd quite like to get into the events side of

things,' he blurted, his hand unwittingly covering his mouth in attempt to stop more words.

Beth smiled.

'Okay. Great. In that case, how about Café Manager and Head Baker's Assistant or something? You could, I don't know, be first contact for celebration cake customers and you can assist me with delivery.' Beth paused, her mind whirring. 'And I can chat to Eve. If she does more events stuff, she could hire you too.'

Pete's eyes widened.

'Yes. Please. I mean, yes, I would like that. Thank you.'

Beth grinned.

'Great. Have a think about the job title and I'll draw up a new job description. We'll go over it tomorrow and get it all sorted. Yeah? And we can talk a new salary.'

Pete nodded.

'Thank you,' he said. 'I mean that. You've been so wonderful to me. I really appreciate the opportunity.'

Beth shook her head.

'You've been heaven sent, Pete. What would I do without you? I want to pay you back, both in whatever career experience you want and in actual money. As much as I can. This business wouldn't have been able to grow like this without you.'

There was an awkward moment as the meeting finished and Pete looked like he was about to hug her but changed his mind. She almost went in for a hug but reminded herself that she was the boss and stopped.

The door opened, the bell above it tinkling, and Beth exhaled in relief. Pete jumped, heading back to the till, smiling as the customer walked through the door.

'Good afternoon. Oh.' He turned to look for Beth.

Beth stared at Glen as Glen's gaze found her.

'Hi,' he said.

'Hello. Are you here for those cakes you keep forgetting to grab?' she asked, heading towards the counter.

'Actually, a favour.'

Beth stopped and studied Glen.

'If you have a moment?' he added.

'Sure.' Beth exchanged a look with Pete.

'I'll have a latte,' Glen told Pete, taking off his coat. 'Is here okay?' he asked Beth, gesturing to a table by the window.

'Sure.'

'Two lattes?' asked Pete as Beth went to join Glen.

'Please. Thank you.' Beth shot Pete another look as she sat down. She refocused on Glen. 'What's this favour?'

'These went quickly last night,' he said, pulling a napkin-wrapped parcel from his pocket and laying it on the table between them. Beth pulled a curious frown. Glen unwrapped the napkin to reveal one of the Nutcracker cookies she'd made for the ghost tour. Beth smiled.

'They always go fast,' she explained.

'I was wondering if you could teach me how to make them?'

Beth stared in horror at Glen.

'You want to learn how to make gingerbread cookies?'

He nodded.

'In the shape of Nutcrackers.'

'But why?' she asked

Glen fidgeted.

'Because Eve and Jeff suggested I enter the baking competition with Rob. Rob likes the Nutcracker.' His gaze flickered up and then away from her.

'He told me you don't like the Nutcracker. You said he was creepy.'

Glen shrugged.

'It's for him, not me.'

'You want me to teach you and him how to make them?'

'No, just me.'

Those three words hung in the air between them as Pete placed their coffees on the table.

'Okay. I need to make gingerbread so, sure. We can do it now if you want?' Beth blinked down at the drink. Her fingertips were tingling, her mind unable to settle on any coherent thought. Trying to make sense of this man was like working to unravel a knot in a string of Christmas lights.

'I can't right now. And I don't want to impose. How about tonight?' Glen offered, sipping his scalding coffee.

Beth nodded.

'Okay. Tonight.' That made more sense. It would give her time to prepare. Her day's list filled her mind along with an impending sense of dread.

'What time would be best?' Glen asked.

'Erm. Eight,' she said apologetically. 'Maybe eat before you come otherwise you'll just fill up on gingerbread.'

Glen's smile did something pleasurable to her insides and she inwardly cursed him. What was he up to?

There was another pause as he sipped his coffee and she stared into hers.

'Were you avoiding me last night?' she asked, not looking up. She didn't want to see the expression on his face, the panic or humour or ignorance. She wasn't sure which would be more painful.

'What? No, of course not.'

Beth risked a glance up and Glen searched her eyes. He tapped two fingers on the table.

'No. I wasn't avoiding you,' he said. 'Eve's good at her job, isn't she. Handled the whole thing like a pro.'

'She is a pro,' said Beth.

'Right. I can see why my dad loved those things so much. The house felt alive.' A sad smile touched his lips for a moment. 'It's nice that she's bringing that back.'

'It is,' Beth murmured.

'Okay, I need to go pick up Rob but I'll buy some cakes while I'm here.' Glen drained his coffee and stood. Beth watched him, her drink completely untouched. 'I'll meet you here at eight?'

The words slowly sank into Beth.

'Oh, no, not here. Everything will be locked up and alarmed by then. Come to mine, I have everything for making gingerbread there. It won't be a professional kitchen but then I guess you'll be using Jeff's kitchen, right?'

Glen handed Beth his phone so she could write down her address and with one of his devilish smiles, he turned away from her to gaze fondly over the cakes she'd made. Pete hovered over him, waiting to pack up his order. Slowly, Beth stood and took her latte towards the kitchen.

'See you tonight, then,' she managed.

'See you at eight,' came Glen's voice.

By the time eight o'clock came around, Beth had made it home in time to shower, have something to eat and prepare the ingredients to make gingerbread biscuits on a clean kitchen worktop. She poured herself a glass of wine and was taking a sip when there was a knock at the door. Not moving, Beth took a deep breath and steadied herself. When she opened the front door she was met by Glen in his long dark coat and red scarf, a hint of that smile of his and a single red rose. She stared at the rose.

'Hi,' she managed.

'Hi.'

She let Glen in, closing the door behind him. He turned back to her and offered her the rose.

'These are surprisingly hard to find. Not the right season, I guess, but I didn't think a sprig of holly would have done the trick.'

Beth looked from the rose to him.

'Trick?'

His eyes softened, a warm smile spreading across his face.

'A thank you, for teaching me how to bake something which I hope is simple.'

Beth laughed and took the rose.

'Well, thank you.'

'I know a bottle of wine is probably more usual in the circumstances but...'

'But?' Beth prompted as Glen shrugged off his coat and scarf, hanging them up on the coat hook Beth gestured to.

'A single red rose is more romantic than a bottle of wine, isn't it. A bottle of wine can mean a lot of things. A rose is straight forward.'

Beth hesitated and looked back to him, opening her mouth, changing her mind and closing it again.

'Can we go through and sit down?' asked Glen as he watched her battle the confusion.

Silently, Beth led him through her small house to the open plan living room-kitchen. Glen sat on the sofa and patted the seat beside him. Carefully, Beth sat with enough distance to allow her to study him. The rose stem was pinched between her fingers, the single sip of wine sizzling through her.

'I know I've been something of an idiot lately,' said Glen, avoiding her gaze. 'I wanted to apologise. Because you were right, I was avoiding you during the ghost tour.'

Beth sagged, staring down at the rose.

'I don't even know why. Rob chastised me afterwards.'

Beth looked up sharply.

'He did? Why?'

Glen slowly looked up into her eyes. His were a soft brown and if he were to put on that smile in that moment she would have melted into the sofa. Maybe she would have melted anyway, if she had the faintest idea of what was going on or what he was thinking.

'He was talking about you quite a lot today. He likes you. And so do I.'

Beth watched him, waiting for more. Glen looked away, glancing back to the kitchen and the bowls of carefully weighed ingredients.

'We should probably get cooking, right?'

'Baking,' Beth corrected. 'Glen, what do you want?'

'Hmm?'

Beth turned so her body faced him.

'I feel like there have been lots of hints dropped

and just when I think I've got this and you figured out, you do something that makes me question it. You kiss me under the mistletoe on Boxing Day after an evening of talking and flirting, and then you vanish back to London even though you said you'd pop to the bakery before you left. Okay, so Rob was sick, I understand that now but you didn't say a word. Then I bump into you at a random wedding and you buy me a drink. I wasn't even a guest. That didn't feel like a normal thing. That felt like maybe it meant something except that then you ignored me at the ghost tour. And the problem is that our kiss on Boxing Day did mean something to me. And honestly, I have no idea if it meant anything to you.' Beth snapped her mouth shut and stared down at the rose still clenched between her fingers. When Glen didn't answer, she stood. 'I should go put this in water. Come on, I'll teach you how to make gingerbread.'

She wandered into the kitchen, holding a vase under the tap and slipping the rose into the water. The vase and rose went onto the window sill, out of the way, and Beth calmly tied on her apron. Glen followed her, scanning the bowls of ingredients she'd laid out. When she glanced back to him, he caught her eye and produced something from his pocket. Placing it on the worktop, he unwrapped the paper around it and revealed a shortbread cookie in the shape of a holly leaf. Beth looked back to him.

'Is that...?'

'One of the holly cookies you made and brought along last Boxing Day,' said Glen. 'I was going to eat it but couldn't bring myself to after I couldn't get to your bakery the next day. A friend of mine offered to preserve it after I told her I was worried it would rot. She coated it in resin.'

'You coated one of my cookies in resin?'

Glen nodded.

'So I could keep it.'

'Why?' Beth breathed. Her stomach churned, wondering whether she should be freaked out or not.

'As a reminder, if nothing else. Of a lovely evening, of that kiss under the mistletoe.' Glen met her eyes. 'As a reminder not to let someone like you slip away from me so easily again. You wanted me to come visit your bakery, right?'

'Of course.' Beth's hand went to her stomach.

'You wanted to see me again.'

'I wanted you to kiss me again,' Beth confessed.

Glen smiled and stepped towards her. Beth's heart raced, after waiting a year for this to happen, it was almost as if it was happening too fast. She couldn't concentrate, she couldn't focus.

The sound of ringing made both of them jump. Glen hesitated and then relented with a huff, pulling his phone from his pocket. He answered, his eyes hard on Beth. She was still breathing hard but this pause gave her time to think. Did she want

Glen to kiss her again, here, in her kitchen? Yes, she did. If she was honest, she wanted him to kiss her hard, to lift her up onto the kitchen worktop, to place his arms around her while her fingers worked through his hair—

'I'll be there in a bit.' Glen's voice broke through the fantasy. Beth blinked up at him.

'Is everything okay? Is Rob okay?'

Glen softened again, smiling at her.

'He's fine. An important client has been trying to call me and it turns out my assistant stupidly gave him the Manor's number. That was Jeff. I've got to go and sort it all out. I'm so sorry.' He gave the ingredients a sad look. 'Maybe I won't enter the competition.'

'Oh.'

'It was really just an excuse to be alone with you,' Glen admitted.

'Oh?'

Glen fretted for a moment. Stay here, willed Beth silently. Forget the client, stay with me. Glen didn't hear her.

'Come to Boxing Day,' he said. 'Eve's probably invited you already anyway but if not then come. Come with me.'

A smile forced its way onto Beth's lips.

'Okay,' she murmured, unsure of where the evening had gone wrong, or even if it had gone wrong. 'You could still enter the competition. Here, take these ingredients. I'll send you instructions.'

'Really?'

'Yeah.'

'It isn't quite the hands in a bowl mixing gingerbread that I had in mind,' Glen murmured, their eyes meeting again. Beth's stomach twisted pleasurably.

'Oh, so that was your plan? We can do it another time.' She grinned.

Glen's gaze moved up and down her, taking her and her mucky apron in.

'It's a date,' he said.

Beth helped him take the ingredients to his car and ordered him to involve Rob. She would send him the instructions later that evening. He promised to do his best and there was an awkward pause as he opened his car door and turned back to her.

'I'm sorry I messed up again,' he said softly. 'This is the last time, I promise.'

Beth tutted.

'Don't make promises you can't keep, Glen Hargreaves.'

Her chest tightened as that roguish smile bloomed on Glen's face. He leaned forward and Beth prepared herself. His cheek brushed hers and his lips placed a soft kiss on her skin. For a moment his breath was in her ear and his cologne was in her nostrils along with the scent of his warm skin. His stubble grazed over her and then he was gone.

Beth shivered as she watched his car disappear

down the road, his warmth still on her cheek. Unable to stop grinning, she skipped back into her house and let out a joyous whoop! as soon as the door was closed.

8

The day before Christmas Eve was dark with thick cloud. It was a good excuse to turn all the Christmas lights on, twinkling fairy lights that ran along the top of each fair stall on the drive, in the gardens and the orchard of the Manor. The stalls had tables covered in silver-edged tablecloths upon which different products were displayed. There were cheeses and mince pies, handcrafted gifts of coloured glass and bright wool, a selection of Christmas trees in one corner being lovingly chosen and bundled up for families late to decorating their home, carved birdhouses and wooden toys, oil paintings from a local artist, and a photographer darting around and pausing to capture different moments. Off to the side was a line of tables which had started the fair empty but were now slowly filling up with baking competition entries. Beth kept an eye on them, trying not to see who was entering what but ensuring they were all safe and untouched. Janine was officially in charge of overseeing them. She took each entry and covered it, ready for tasting. The crowds had come early, with some lining up at the gate before the opening time. Eve had gone around and checked all of the stall-holders were ready before she opened the gates ten minutes early.

Beth had her own stall which she was manning with help from Pete. He was a better salesman than her, it turned out, so she soon found herself letting him take over so she could grab Eve for a chat or dart away for a hot chocolate. All the while, she kept an eye out for Glen and Rob, but saw neither.

'Hey, wedding cake baker.'

Beth turned until she found the owner of the voice. It took her a moment to recognise the wedding planner but when she did they both grinned at one another as Simon reached her.

'Hey,' Beth greeted him.

Simon glanced around the fair. He had a paper bag stuffed with woollen purchases and he did a double take at Beth's own cake stall. 'This fair is really something, isn't it. Did you say your friend organised this whole thing? I wish this had happened at the beginning of December, I could have done all my Christmas shopping here.'

'Good feedback,' said Beth. 'And yes, Eve Dutton put all of this together. It's impressive, isn't it? She's got a passion for it.'

Simon's eyes were still on Beth's cake stall.

'And she wants to get into weddings?'

'Perhaps. Shall I go find her? And you can have a cake while you wait,' Beth offered. Simon's eyes lit up.

'Perfect.'

Beth introduced him to Pete. It didn't go unnoticed that Pete's eyes widened as he said hello to Simon, his cheeks flushing a little. Beth smiled to herself before telling Simon to help himself to a cake while she went searching for Eve.

'Eve. Eve. You remember that wedding planner?' Beth said in a rush, a little out of breath as she reached Eve in the orchard chatting to a stallholder.

'Yeah? Yes?'

'He's here, very impressed and wants a chat.'

Eve stared at Beth as this sank in and then politely excused herself from her conversation with the stallholder. Beth led her back to Pete and Simon at a fast walk.

'He's impressed?' Eve hissed.

'Very. Wanted to know if you're interested in planning weddings.'

Eve made a strange squeaking noise and then, out of habit, checked the time on her phone.

'Baking competition starts in thirty minutes,' she told Beth. Beth nodded and slowed as her own stall came into sight. Simon and Pete were deep in conversation and a part of Beth didn't want to interrupt.

'Do they know each other?' Eve whispered, slowing next to Beth.

'Literally just met.'

'Cute.' Eve smiled, digging her elbow into Beth. 'You know, I think there's something about this house at Christmas.'

'You think?' Beth dug her elbow into Eve in retaliation. 'Come on.' Beth approached cautiously. 'Simon?'

Simon turned and smiled at Beth, his gaze landing on Eve.

'This is Eve, the magical creator of this fair.' Beth almost did a dramatic bow to show Eve off but thought better of it, dipping away as Simon turned his full attention to Eve.

'So pleased to meet you,' said Simon, shaking Eve's hand. 'Beth tells me you might be interested in organising weddings?'

'Erm, yes, maybe, I think so,' Eve stammered.

'Can we have a chat?' asked Simon. He glanced back to Beth and Pete as he wandered away, throwing Pete a smile.

Beth caught Pete sighing as he watched them walk away.

'Like him, do you?'

'He was nice,' said Pete, busying himself with tidying the stall.

'Did you get his number?'

'Nope.'

'How come?'

'Because I'm an idiot,' said Pete, straightening the tablecloth. 'Plus he lives in London and I don't fancy commuting for a relationship. Double plus he's gorgeous and probably has a boyfriend.'

'You don't know that,' Beth told him gently.

'Nope. No, I don't,' said Pete, his mouth twisting. 'I should go get his number, shouldn't I.'

'I would,' said Beth. 'But be quick or do it later because I have a baking competition to judge and if we leave these cakes unattended they'll be none left when we get back.'

Eve still hadn't re-emerged thirty minutes later so Beth made her way over to the baking competition tables on her own. Janine was waiting for her.

'How's it looking?'

'Amazing,' said Janine. 'I'm glad I'm not judging.'

Beth smiled, glancing over the entries.

'Where's Eve?' Janine asked.

'No idea. She's talking to a wedding planner I met a little while ago.'

'Oh.' Janine's eyes lit up. 'Did she propose to Jeff?'

'Oh, no, she's talking about becoming a wedding planner.'

Janine's face fell.

'Oh. Right, of course. She'd be brilliant at it.'

Beth looked back into the fair.

'She absolutely would,' she murmured.

Beth helped Janine set up for the competition and took her place at the end of the tables. With a few minutes to go, Eve rushed over, a grin stretching from ear to ear, and apologised for being late.

'How did it go?' asked Beth.

'Brilliantly. Tell you later,' said Eve, taking the P.A. system's microphone from Janine and announcing to the fair that the baking competition was about to be judged. Beth sat back in the chair Janine had provided. A small crowd began to gather, people pointing out their entries on the table. Beth tried not to look, she didn't want to be biased by knowing who had baked what. A couple of regulars waved to her, she waved back but refused to look at the table of dishes.

'Judging begins in two minutes,' Eve's voice bounced around the fair. 'You have sixty seconds to get your entry to the table. Quick now.'

Eve jumped as Jeff appeared by her side, kissing her cheek and then giving Beth a thumbs up. Frowning curiously, Beth gave him a thumbs up back.

'Wait! Hold on!'

The crowd parted a little and Glen, red-faced and panting, came running up to the table with a foil-covered plate. He stopped in front of Beth, flashed her an exhausted grin and laid the plate on the table.

'Sorry I'm late,' he managed as Rob appeared behind him.

Beth smiled.

'Better late than never.'

'I think that's becoming the mantra I live by,' Glen muttered as Janine took his entry. His soft eyes met Beth's and she waved him away.

'Go recover. I can't know whose is whose.'

Her insides twisted, sending a jolt of pleasure down her body as Glen winked at her and then leaned on Jeff. His younger brother led him over to the side where Glen collapsed into a chair and caught his breath. Rob had disappeared but Beth didn't have a chance to look for him. The judging was beginning.

'Let's start the baking competition judging, shall we?' boomed Eve's voice. 'We are thrilled that Beth Adams of Flour Power Bakery, on the high street, has agreed to be our judge. First prize is one hundred pounds and a free celebration cake from Flour Power Bakery. Second prize is fifty pounds and a box of cupcakes from Flour Power Bakery. Third prize is twenty-five pounds and a ten pound Flour Power Bakery gift card. Have I said Flour Power Bakery enough, Beth?'

Beth laughed and nodded to Eve as a chuckle ran through the crowd.

'Let's begin!' said Eve to a round of applause and cheers.

Beth stood and began at one end of the long line of tables. The crowd watched but were, thankfully, not silent. The Christmas music was still playing across the fair, people were chatting, somewhere someone roared with laughter. Some children ran through the crowds, giggling as they went.

The first entry was a plate of mince pies. Beth tasted one and closed her eyes as something that she hadn't baked filled her senses. It was delicious. This was going to be harder than she thought. The second entry was a plate of white chocolate and cranberry muffins which was strange but somehow worked perfectly. The third was a large celebration cake decorated in fondant to represent a sprig of holly. Beth sliced through it revealing layers of green sponge and white buttercream. She could only take small bites of each thing, which felt like a waste until she saw Janine, Eve and Jeff behind her helping to polish off what was left before the untouched remains were given back to the entrant.

There were more mince pies in different types of pastry, a cranberry pie which was unfortunately more bitter than sweet, heaps of gooey brownies, chocolate logs thick with icing, apple pies that melted in the mouth, wobbly gingerbread houses constructed with love, layered cakes with gold icing and one beautifully designed as a snow globe, cup-cakes, biscuits, the variety was stunning. Beth reached a plate and stopped. On the plate were seven gingerbread biscuits that, if she squinted and tilted her head, almost looked like Nutcrackers. Her chest tightened and before she could stop herself, her eyes were up searching for Glen. She spotted him in the corner, arms crossed against his broad chest, his slight belly beneath, and a worried twitch at the edge of his mouth. The biscuits were warped and perhaps rushed but Beth snapped the arm from one and popped it into her mouth.

'Good texture,' she told Janine who wrote down the notes on her clipboard. 'Good flavour. Design is... Well, they tried hard.' She kept her eyes on Glen as she swallowed the gingerbread. A smile forced its way onto his face.

'How are they?' Jeff asked quietly.

'Shush,' Eve hissed.

'Oh, come on, she's staring right at him. She knows they're his.' Jeff reached across and took the armless gingerbread Nutcracker from the plate, snapping off a leg and passing it to Eve to try.

In the end Beth had a terrible time of choosing a winner. She wanted to give the family who had built a wonky gingerbread house something but the snow globe and celebration cakes were incredible, not to mention that apple pie. In the end, she bargained with Eve and gave out joint prizes. The gingerbread house came third, much to the delight of the family of five who had made it, a layered celebration cake and a chocolate log took second place and that snow globe and apple pie took joint first place. Beth explained how difficult judging had been and how she hoped none of them got any ideas of starting their own bakery on the high street, then passed Eve the microphone so she could announce the end of the fair.

Beth's body relaxed as she stepped away,

reaching for the plate of Nutcrackers and finding a quiet spot to herself.

'You'll definitely need a drink with those,' came Glen's voice. Beth looked up and smiled as he approached with two paper cups of beer. 'You really shouldn't eat them. I was worried about you just taking one bite.'

'Why? They're delicious. You understand why I couldn't place you, though, right?' Beth took the beer he offered and they settled down together on a bench so recently vacated that the wood was still warm.

'Yeah, they're awful.'

'I couldn't be seen to be biased,' Beth corrected.

Glen laughed.

'Oh yeah, otherwise you'd have put them first, right?'

Beth offered him the plate of his own biscuits. He gave her a look until she said, 'Go on, try one.'

He took a biscuit and the smallest bite. His features lightened as he chewed.

'Actually not that bad.'

'No, they're delicious. You just need to work on your decoration, that's all. That's my fault, I didn't teach you any of that.'

Glen watched her silently for a moment, his gaze lingering on her lips. She hesitated, wondering if she was about to get a gingerbread flavoured kiss.

'Does the Nutcracker still freak you out?' she murmured, looking up at him.

'He does. But you like him,' said Glen softly.

Beth smiled.

'I thought you made these because Rob liked him?'

Glen cursed under his breath and then laughed.

'Well, there you go. You caught me. Rob used to like the Nutcracker when he was little but not anymore. Now he prefers cars, guitars and people his own age.'

Beth grinned.

'You made them for me,' she breathed.

Glen searched her eyes.

'I came back for you,' he said, leaning towards her. Beth echoed him and just as their lips were about to touch, her skin tingling with anticipated pleasure, there came the call of, 'Glen? Beth?'

They jumped apart and looked around. The crowd of the fair was dispersing, only a few families were left now along with the friends and staff of the Manor and the stallholders packing away their wares.

'Beth?' Janine caught sight of them and beckoned them over. Curious, Beth and Glen exchanged a glance and stood, taking their biscuits and beer with them.

'We're going back to that moment,' Glen whispered in her ear. Beth's heart thudded as she nodded. They ended up outside the front of the Manor and she made sure she stood just a little too close to Glen so that his arm brushed against her.

There was a shuffling and then the feel of his fingers against her back. A shudder of warmth moved through her body.

Jeff had Eve's hand and was leading her over to the porch, glancing around at the small crowd.

'Eve,' he started, clearing his throat and wringing his hands after he positioned her on the porch. Eve was staring at him with wide eyes. It dawned on Beth what was about to happen and she shoved the plate of Nutcrackers into Glen's hand so that she could cover her mouth and keep her reaction in. 'Eve, almost exactly a year ago to the hour we stood here, on this porch, under a sprig of mistletoe and had our first kiss. The last year has been...' Jeff sighed, biting his lip against the grin. 'Magic. Because you are magic. You brought magic into my father's life, you brought it into this house and now you've filled my life with it. And I don't want that to stop. Ever. I want my life to be filled with your magic and I want to make you as happy as you've made me. I want to be here for you as you've been here for me.'

A quiet gasp ran through the crowd as Jeff got down on one knee.

'Eve Dutton, will you marry me?'

Beth was bouncing on the balls of her feet, something she only became aware of when she realised Glen was watching her and not his brother's proposal. Beth resisted the urge to look up at Glen, keeping her eyes on Eve as her friend nodded and wrapped her arms around Jeff's neck. The crowd cheered and applauded as Jeff swung Eve round, lips pressed against hers. When Jeff let her go, Eve squealed and searched the crowd for Beth. Glen took Beth's beer so they could run towards each other. Beth held Eve tight.

'Finally,' she murmured. Eve giggled.

'You'll make the cake, right?'

9

Beth had spent Christmas Eve and Christmas Day too busy to think but even so, whenever she stopped, the thought of Glen would push its way through. Glen and that near kiss. Glen and his gingerbread Nutcracker biscuits. Glen and his broad frame and the sense of safety whenever he was next to her. When her mother had suggested she stay for Boxing Day, she'd been forced to tell her everything. Her mother had smiled, hand over her heart, and told Beth she had to go to the Manor for Boxing Day. Beth promised she'd spend the following week back with her family, packed her bags and popped home for a shower and change of clothes before rushing up to the Manor.

This time last year, she'd walked into the Manor behind Eve wondering what on earth she was doing. She'd brought mince pies and biscuits, been introduced to Jeff's family, and there had been a soft silence in the house as they'd mourned Stanley Hargreaves. His father's death had hit Glen hard and he'd been in no mood for talking when Beth had first attempted to start a conversation. She'd ended up watching the television with Rob instead until she caught Glen swooning over her mince pies. That had been the ice breaker she'd needed to engage in adult conversation and once Glen had a couple of mince pies and a few glasses of wine in him, he'd begun to open up. No wonder they'd ended up underneath the mistletoe on the porch, watching their breath cloud against the cold air as they took a break from being surrounded by people.

Beth hesitated as she went to knock on the Manor's front door. Glancing up at the mistletoe, she smiled. She'd glanced up at it on a late Boxing Day last year, somehow at the same time that Glen had also glanced up. Their eyes had met, the world spinning a little as Glen had stepped forward and placed his lips on hers. It had been a somewhat drunken first kiss but unlike any other drunken kiss Beth had experienced. It had been enough to stay with her for a whole year, almost a forgotten, faded memory until Glen had walked around the corner and straight into her at the wedding.

Beth took a deep breath and knocked on the door. Eve answered, a grin plastered to her face and a sparkling diamond ring on her finger which she immediately showed to Beth. Beth did the usual crooning and gasping expected and then passed a box of mince pies to her friend. Eve barely noticed, she was so caught up in the day, talking non-stop about who was there, what was happening, how her day had been, how wonderful Christmas had been.

'Did you have a good Christmas?'

Beth blinked, Eve's words finally breaking through.

'Yeah, it was lovely. I have a Christmas cake here.' She showed Eve a second box that she was carrying beneath a tray of shortbread biscuits.

'Oh, Beth. You spoil us.' Eve, unable to grin further or clap her hands, did a little skip. 'The yule log you made me was incredible. We shared some with Glen, Wendy and the kids, of course, but kept half just for us.' Eve winked.

Beth laughed.

'I don't want to know what you two get up to with my yule logs.'

Eve gave her a playful look and led her through the house and into the kitchen. As she walked past the living room, Beth glanced through and somehow managed to catch Glen's eye as he peered through the doorway. Had he been waiting for her? Or had he simply heard her voice?

'You never did tell me about what happened with Simon, the wedding planner,' Beth murmured as she walked into the kitchen to find Wendy, the middle Hargreaves child, preparing some roast potatoes. Wendy smiled at Beth in such a way that suggested she knew something. Beth narrowed her eyes.

'Hi, Wendy.'

'Beth. Did you have a good Christmas?'

'Yes, thanks. You?'

Wendy nodded.

'It was quiet. My first Christmas as a single mother.' She gave a short laugh. 'Jeff and Eve kindly invited us here but I wanted to get that first Christmas over with, you know? It went better than expected.'

'That must have been tough. I'm glad you're here now. Are your kids here too?' Beth hadn't heard the telltale noise of children.

'No, they're with their dad today and tomorrow.' Wendy sighed. 'It's a weird feeling. Somewhere between relaxing and wondering what I've forgotten all the time.'

Beth smiled.

'Well, I've brought mince pies, shortbread and Christmas cake, if that helps?'

Wendy's eyes widened.

'You know, I've been thinking about your mince pies all year. They'll definitely fill the gap.'

Beth looked around the kitchen and then out of the doorway before sneakily opening the box with the mince pies and offering them to Wendy. Wendy glanced at Eve and took one mince pie, biting into it immediately and closing her eyes.

'They live up to the memory,' she said around the mouthful. 'Thank you.'

'Anytime,' said Beth. 'So? Wedding planner?' She turned back to Eve.

'Simon asked if I wanted to buy his business,' said Eve.

'What? No franchise, no joint partners, no delegating to you?' Beth leaned back against a worktop, taking this in.

'Nope. A straight up buy my business deal.'

'How much?'

'Not as much as you'd think. I'd be buying a couple of booked weddings from him, if the clients want to continue, and a list of suppliers. Not including a baker, I told him I have one of those.' Eve raised a questioning eyebrow at Beth.

'You know I'd love to be your go-to wedding cake maker,' Beth told her. 'Especially now that Pete has been promoted. He's told me he'd love to be more involved in the events side, so I know he'd be happy to help and get involved. He hit it off with Simon, I'm hoping he doesn't run off to London now to see more of him.'

Eve gasped.

'That would be amazing. Not for you, obviously.' Beth shrugged.

'Life happens,' she said. 'You're going to buy the business?'

'I can't afford it,' Eve admitted. 'I can afford half of it.' She drifted off, staring at Beth. Beth blinked.

'What are you saying?'

'I'm suggesting that you buy the other half and we become partners.'

Beth grimaced but then images of wedding cakes

floated through her mind. Of all the things she truly loved making, decorating a wedding cake was at the top of her list.

'Maybe,' she said. 'I'll think about it.'

Eve agreed.

'Okay. Sure. Probably the wrong day to ask anyway. Today is for relaxing and celebrating and eating roast potatoes and cake.'

Wendy smiled at Eve, turning back to face the friends.

'You know, Jeff might be keen to invest,' she suggested. 'Or Glen. Glen did a lot of investing in his younger days.' She glanced at Beth. 'Or, you know, maybe I could invest.'

Eve considered this.

'A family partnership,' she murmured.

'Exactly,' said Wendy.

'What's this? What plans are you concocting?' asked Jeff as he walked into the kitchen. Glen followed with an empty glass.

'Business plans,' Eve told him, unable to keep the smile from her face as Jeff snaked an arm around her waist. 'The wedding planning business.'

Jeff looked between Eve, Beth and Wendy.

'That could work,' he murmured, grinning at his sister.

Beth looked sideways at Glen as he poured himself another glass of wine.

'Did I see you come in with mince pies?' he asked quietly, just between the two of them.

Beth opened the box and offered him one.

'But don't tell anyone,' she whispered back, aware that everyone was watching them. Glen laughed and took a bite.

Jeff poured Beth a drink and she remained by Glen's side, unsure of what else to do with herself. The kitchen was full and warm, and eventually Wendy demanded that everyone leave so she could cook in peace.

They traipsed into the living room and there was a knock at the door as Janine, Harry and Dave, the Manor's gardeners, arrived. Jeff and Eve went to see them in and get them drinks, leaving Beth with Glen and Rob, on the sofas in front of the television.

'Turn that off now, Rob,' said Glen. 'Time to chat before dinner.'

Rob did as he was told and there was a silence between the three of them. A warmth spread through Beth's chest as she watched father and son for a moment. This could be it, she thought. This is what life could be like.

The thought was broken by the newly arrived guests descending on them with loud voices and demands for Beth's mince pies.

10

After a wonderful meal cooked entirely by Wendy, before Beth's Christmas cake made an appearance, the family and their friends settled back with full bellies in front of the fire.

'No snow this year,' said Harry.

'There's time yet,' said Jeff, his arm around Eve who was slowly falling asleep, her cheek against his chest.

Beth watched her friend, the diamond on her finger catching her eye as it glistened in the firelight. Slowly, she got up and placed down her drink, making her way out of the room.

'Everything okay?' asked Eve, eyes suddenly open.

'Going to the bathroom. If I'm not back in half an hour, I've fallen into a food coma and you're to come wake me up with cake,' Beth told her.

Eve settled back into Jeff's arms, a contented smile on her face as her eyes closed again.

Beth didn't go to the bathroom. Instead, she

quietly opened the front door and stood out on the porch. Harry was right, there was no snow and it was too dark to see what the clouds above were like. There were definitely clouds, Beth couldn't see a single star but she could feel the heaviness. She sniffed and wondered if that heavy scent was a promise. Filling her lungs with the chill night air, she leaned back against the wood of the porch, her mind drifting.

'This isn't the bathroom,' whispered Glen, making her jump as he softly closed the door behind him.

'Don't creep up on me,' she told me, hand over her heart. 'Scared the life out of me.'

He smiled playfully.

'Sorry. Next time I'll knock.'

She gave him a look.

'I think the lights are still up around the orchard,' said Glen, peering around her. 'Do you want to go see?'

Beth's heart jumped sending something exquisite through her body.

'Sure.' She shrugged, wrapping her arms around her and stepping off the porch. Glen looked her up and down before vanishing back into the house. 'Or not?' she called softly after him.

He reappeared with their coats and she gratefully pulled hers on. It was one thing standing on the porch by the heat of the house and another walking down to the darkness of the orchard.

'Have you flicked the light switch?' she asked as Glen led the way onto the driveway and over the gravel.

'I have,' said Glen, pausing so she could catch up.

As they walked towards the glow of the orchard, with the fairy lights still obviously up and working, the backs of their hands brushed against one another. Glen's finger reached out and curled around her little finger. Smiling to herself, Beth took his hand in hers and he gave her a gentle squeeze. No words were spoken. Beth wasn't sure she could remember how to form words as her mind whirred, her body tingling.

Glen led her into the orchard and they paused, taking in the sight of the fairy lights twirling up each apple and pear tree.

'We should spend more of Christmas here,' Beth breathed. 'It's beautiful without a crowd.'

Glen found the bench over to the side and sat, patting the space beside him for Beth. She sat slowly, wondering if she was sitting too close but unable to make herself move away. He didn't seem to mind. They sat in silence for a moment, taking in the lights and stillness of the trees. A shiver ran through Beth as a breeze picked up. She pulled her coat tighter and shoved her hands into her pockets.

'I'll be quick,' said Glen.

Beth turned to him sharply.

'What?'

Glen struggled for a moment and then pulled

something out of his pocket. Beth exhaled in a cloud as she realised it was a wrapped gift. Her eyes lifted to his.

'You bought me something?'

He nodded.

'I saw it and thought of you.'

Beth bit her lip as her insides somersaulted. Pulling her hands from her pockets, she took the gift.

'You really didn't have to.'

'I know,' he said, watching her. 'Open it.'

With shaking fingers, Beth clumsily unwrapped the present. It had been beautifully done and she couldn't help but wonder if he'd had it gift-wrapped in a shop. Inside the green and gold paper was a box. She glanced up, smiling. The tape gave way under her fingernails and inside the box, under a layer of tissue, was a pristine and beautifully made glass ornament of red and black.

Beth laughed, looking up into Glen's smile

'You bought me a Nutcracker.'

He nodded as she carefully removed the soldier from the box, holding it up against the fairy lights.

'It's a tree ornament,' he told her, his voice low as if the words were a secret, just for her.

'It's beautiful,' she breathed as the light twinkled through the glass. Her chest tightened, tears pricking her eyes. 'I love it. Thank you.'

Glen leaned closer.

'Will you think of me when you look at it?'

Beth smiled.

'Honestly? I think about you now whenever I see a Nutcracker.' She turned to find Glen's face close to hers. Carefully, barely looking, she placed the ornament back into the box.

'I do sort of wish they weren't called Nutcrackers,' Glen murmured, his eyes on her lips.

Beth gave a soft laugh and for a moment, the tips of their noses touched.

'I sort of wish I didn't have to look at a Nutcracker to be reminded of you,' she breathed back. His eyes lifted to hers. 'I sort of wish I could just look at you,' she added, her mouth dry, heart racing.

The corners of his mouth lifted into a slow smile and he gave a slight shake of his head.

'I don't know what it is,' he said. 'If it's your eyes or your smile or the way you always smell of cake or just the thought of how soft your hands are underneath the flour and icing, but I just can't...' He drifted off, lowering his eyes again.

'Can't what?' asked Beth, holding her breath, readying herself for this to go horribly wrong.

'Resist you,' Glen finished, his eyes back on hers. 'I tried. Kept telling myself I didn't want anything serious, that it's better to just be me and my son, but... He's nearly grown up and I just can't resist you.'

Beth didn't even try to stop the grin spreading over her face. She leaned closer until her lips grazed over his.

'Then don't,' she murmured.

'Come to London with me,' he said, the words spilling out fast in an exhale. She searched his eyes, the tips of their noses bumping again.

'Sometimes,' she agreed. 'If you come here sometimes and take me away from my kitchen.'

Glen smiled.

'I can work with that,' he murmured. One of his arms had moved around the back of her and now lay gently against her lower back and waist. 'We'll work it out.'

'Promise,' said Beth without thinking, her eyes already closing.

'Promise,' said Glen as his lips met hers.

The kiss was soft at first as they felt their way. Then it deepened, became a little harder. Glen took the gift from Beth's lap and placed it at their feet before wrapping his arms around her. Her hands were in his hair, holding him close. The scent of his cologne filled her senses, along with the tingle of his warmth against her chill, the tenderness of his lips, the feel of his slight stubble as her fingers brushed over his cheek.

As they parted, Glen kept his arms around her and Beth let one hand slide down his arm. He watched her and she wondered if they were thinking the same thing. He took her hand in his, rubbing her cold fingertips.

'We should do that more often,' he said.

She nodded.

'We should.'

'I'm sorry I didn't do that a year ago.'

'You did,' Beth pointed out. 'On the porch, under the mistletoe.'

Glen sighed.

'Copying my brother.' He looked down at their entwined hands. 'Because I wasn't sure what else to do. This is more me.' He glanced around the orchard.

'And me,' said Beth. Glen looked back to her.

'I don't have to stay in London for work,' he told her.

'We can figure it out,' she assured him.

'And I won't be proposing to you here on this spot in a year's time.'

'Oh?'

'No. It'll be somewhere different, when you're not expecting it.'

Beth laughed and Glen lifted her hand and pressed it to his lips.

'Beth? Glen? Are you out here?' Eve's voice made Beth flinch, her grip on Glen tightening. She looked at him with widening eyes. 'Cake time!' Eve called.

'Well, going back in is going to be awkward,' Beth told Glen with a smile. 'I reckon they all know where we've been.'

Glen searched her eyes.

'Let's stay out here a little longer then,' he told her, pulling her closer.

'You don't want any cake?'

Glen gave a slight shrug.

'I'm hoping that one of the benefits of this happening is that I don't have to wait until Christmas to eat cake made by you.'

Beth grinned as her mind settled, that pleasant, tingling warmth spreading throughout her entire body until it reached her fingertips. She put her arms around Glen's neck and moved forward for another kiss.

Just before their lips met, something cold and wet hit her head. They both looked up.

'Can't be,' Glen murmured.

Beth held out her hands and then looked up at him.

'Do we go in and tell them it's starting to snow?'

Glen's eyes twinkled in the fairy lights.

'Nah.' He leaned in, pulled her close and kissed her as she smiled against his lips. Let the others find them. For now, this was their world. Just the warmth of one another, a glass Nutcracker, twinkling lights among the fruit trees and the first snowflakes of the season.

All's Fair In Love And Christmas

JENNIFER NICE

1

Looking at the time had become less of a habit and more of a compulsion. Wendy had one hour to go before she had to leave the office to pick her children up from school. One hour. She could get a lot done in an hour. Then she'd leave the office and make her way back to her car, parked a short Tube ride away. After picking the children up, she'd make them something to eat and sort out her daughter's homework. Her son needed socks. She mustn't forget the socks. His Christmas bag still needed packing. Wendy always had to time packing his bag otherwise he'd empty it and wear everything just before going to his father's. The divorce had been the right thing to do but sometimes she remembered a simpler life when there weren't so many bags to pack. A couple of years ago, two weeks before Christmas, Wendy had been sitting in this chair, at this desk, contemplating Christmas presents and buying a tree. This year she was that woman who walked into the Tube station muttering, 'Socks,' under her breath.

She sighed and checked the clock.

Fifty-five minutes to go.

'Wendy? Can I have a moment?'

Wendy hid the jump of fright well, she thought. She smiled up at her boss and stood, following him into his office. She closed the door behind her and sat opposite him, his desk between them. There was always that moment of anxiety before he spoke. Why had she been summoned? Was this about the promotion? Was he about to promote her now?

'Are you all ready for Christmas?' Graham asked nonchalantly. He was around fifteen years her senior and while he would say his hair was pepper flecked with salt, it was definitely now more salt than pepper. His fingernails were short from where he bit them, something that had driven Wendy mad when she'd first joined the firm. Sitting in a meeting with a client next to a man who bit his nails had slowly become infuriating. It was a bad habit, he told her once, that had replaced the worse habit of smoking. After that, she didn't feel able to complain about it.

'Yes. Getting there,' she told him.

He nodded, tapping at the desk. The man always needed something to keep his hands busy. She watched distractedly. When was he going to get to the point?

'I think I'm actually going to have Christmas off this year.' Graham gave something of a laugh. 'We'll have filled the partner position by then, so I'm hoping we can all relax a little.'

Wendy nodded. Yes, the partner position. Is that why she was here? It was why she was here generally, in the building. It was why she'd taken this role. Just over ten years spent working cases, paying her dues, all so that she could make partner. This was going to be her year. It had to be.

'Claire's booked us a holiday. Which will be nice. Skiing. I can't stand it but I do like the idea of relaxing with a brandy surrounded by snowy mountains over Christmas.'

Wendy nodded again. Smile and nod, smile and nod, get on with it, man!

'The kids are happy but she left it late to book. It's been expensive.' Graham sighed. 'Do you have your kids this year?'

Wendy shook her head.

'With their father this year?' he continued before she could open her mouth. 'Divorce is a bitch. I should know, I was a divorce lawyer when I started out. Did I ever tell you that?'

Wendy nodded.

'You did,' she said. Multiple times, usually while a bit tipsy at the office Christmas party. He'd offered to help her when he'd heard about her divorce but she preferred to keep the whole thing out of the office.

'Do you have Christmas plans without them?'

'I'm going to my brother's,' said Wendy. 'He

owns our old childhood home now—'

'Oh, that glorious old house out in the sticks?' Graham interrupted.

'Yes—'

'Wonderful. That sounds very festive. And relaxing, I hope? Does he have children?'

Wendy shook her head.

'No, he—'

'Nice and relaxing,' said Graham.

Wendy sighed inaudibly. Usually she'd put up a fight when Graham got into this state of cutting her off. Usually she'd call him on it, tell him to get on with it, tell him to let her get a word in. Usually she'd stick up for herself. This time, however, the words wouldn't come. Somewhere, in her head, that voice that usually broke forth at times like this was too exhausted to find the words. Her gaze drifted down to her black, flat shoes. They were more comfortable than heels but not as comfortable as trainers. She probably only had around thirty minutes left by now, once she got out of here she could swap the shoes for the trainers in her bag. As she shifted, her trouser leg lifted, showing off black sock underneath.

She had to pack her son's socks. Would he have enough? Of course he would, the boy hated wearing socks. Where did he get that from?

'Sue's off sick today, you know?' came Graham's voice.

'Hmm, I heard.' Wendy had fond memories of

wearing thick, fluffy socks in winter, sitting by the open fire of the Manor. Her father would ask her if her feet were too hot, that she should move or take the socks off, but she never wanted to do either so she'd lie and say she was fine.

'Flu, she thinks. She'll be off the rest of the week, so we probably won't see her again until the New Year,' said Graham.

'Oh, that's a shame.' Sure, sitting with sweaty toes wasn't pleasant but her son was rarely sitting in front of a fire wearing thick, fluffy socks. Still, he always complained his feet were too hot. Were her feet always too hot? She wiggled her toes in her shoes.

'Which rather throws the Christmas fair into a dilemma,' said Graham. 'She was organising it with one of our juniors. He kindly volunteered to help.'

Her toes didn't feel hot. The action of wiggling them reminded her of being warm, in bed. A wave of exhaustion washed over her.

'And, of course, we can't cancel the fair. It's on in a week and so important to our reputation. The marketing team have already done the PR. All those people we don't want to disappoint.'

He must get it from his father, Wendy decided. Her ex-husband had always had hot feet in bed. She'd loved it when they'd first gotten together. For a while there, right at the beginning, he'd let her warm her cold feet on him during the winter nights. Something in Wendy's chest ached.

'So, we need a new volunteer to organise the Christmas fair and I realised I know just the person. You, Wendy. So, I'll introduce you to James and you can get acquainted. Yes?'

There was a pause. A silence that filled the room and infiltrated Wendy's thoughts. She blinked and looked up.

'Sorry?'

'You'll finish organising the Christmas fair with James,' said Graham.

Wendy was certain there was a question mark missing.

'I have a pretty heavy caseload at the moment, Graham.'

'Sue's already done most of the organising. It won't take you much time. And there's only a week to go. It'll be over before you know it. And you said you're ready for Christmas, kids aren't with you, so less to prepare, right?'

'That's not really—'

'The Christmas fair is on Friday afternoon. We're making our final decision about who becomes partner at the end of Friday. Right before we close for the year. So once the fair is over, you can go home, grab your bags and head to your brother's. What a great way to finish the year.'

Wendy hesitated, her tired mind desperately trying to work out why he'd slipped in the part about the promotion.

'Graham.'

'I've already checked your cases. Nothing's closing this week. You should be fine.'

'Graham, does my organising this fair have any impact on whether I get the promotion?'

Another pause, this one heavier than the last as Graham's eyes lifted to meet hers.

'Of course not,' he told her. 'We couldn't do that.'

Wendy let the silence fill the room until Graham smiled.

'I'll introduce you to James now, shall I?'

She blinked.

'James?'

'The junior who'll be helping you. He was helping Sue. He'll catch you up and you can delegate to him. See, I told you it'd be easy.'

'Graham—'

He was already up, walking towards the door and beckoning for Wendy to follow. Once out in the main open office, she could hardly raise her voice and make accusations, so she followed silently. This was an opportunity to gather her thoughts, which is why her eyes were down and she nearly bumped into Graham when he stopped.

'James, this is Wendy Winshaw—'

'Hargreaves.'

'Hmm?'

'I've reverted to my maiden name,' said Wendy, still trying to corral some logical, sensible thoughts.

'Right. This is Wendy Hargreaves, one of our senior associates. She'll be taking over from Sue. I want you to catch her up and help her in any way you can. Let's make this fair a great one.' Graham grinned at them both.

Wendy finally lifted her gaze, looking from Graham to this junior called James. He wasn't what she'd been expecting. When she'd heard "junior" she'd conjured up a mental image of a young person, perhaps in their early twenties, straight out of university. This man could pass for late twenties but there was something about him that screamed thirties. Something grown up, something more mature, a certain look about his dark eyes. While the other juniors wore suit jackets, James had removed his and rolled his sleeves up. His arms were muscular and covered with thick, dark hair. That was not something Wendy should have been noticing. She looked back up into those dark eyes and he smiled at her, holding out a hand.

'Pleasure to be working with you,' he said in a smooth voice. He was clean shaven but the afternoon was becoming late and stubble was already making its way back to his chin. He smelled of coffee but there was still a whiff of cologne or aftershave about him.

'And you,' said Wendy, all rational, logical thoughts so carefully processed on the walk over were forgotten. She shook his hand and he gave hers a small squeeze that twisted her stomach. She tried to blink the feelings away.

'Excellent,' said Graham. 'I'll leave you two to it.'

Wendy opened her mouth to protest but Graham had already left, finding someone to drag with him in a loud conversation so she couldn't call him back.

'You sod,' she muttered.

'What's that?'

Wendy turned back to James and attempted a smile.

'Nothing. Nothing.'

'Okay.' James cleared his throat, looking away. 'Do you want to go through the fair plans now?' He looked back to his desk.

Wendy pulled her phone from her pocket and checked the time. She sighed.

'Sorry, I have to dash. Can we do it first thing tomorrow? When do you get in?'

'Eight.'

Wendy blinked. Eight in the morning. She remembered what she used to be able to get into the office at eight in the morning. In the days before the children. In the days before the husband, even.

'Okay, half nine?' she asked. 'Let's get together and go through it then.'

James nodded.

'Sure. Half nine tomorrow.'

There was an awkward pause as James sank back into his chair and Wendy realised she was standing there for no good reason.

'Right. Great. Thanks. See you then.' She swiftly turned on her heel and marched away, her chest and cheeks burning. She wiggled her toes as she walked and there it was, a bit of sweat. She almost laughed. As if she had time right now for butterflies in her stomach and staring at men who might possibly be quite attractive. Christmas was in just over a week, her workload had potentially just doubled and she still had to pack her son's socks.

2

Wendy had been dressed in one of her many smart suits, navy blue with a stylish red jacket, and ready for forty-five minutes but that didn't mean they were close to leaving the house that morning. She folded her nine-year-old son's clothes and placed them gently in a bag while he argued with her.

'I don't want to wear socks today.'

'You'll get cold feet,' Wendy told him.

'No I won't.'

'It's December, Oliver. And you only have one more week of school left.'

'So, one more week of wearing socks?'

'I tell you what,' said Wendy. 'You can take your socks off as soon as you get home, if you like. See how long your feet stay warm, yeah?'

Oliver gave this some thought and while he did, Wendy congratulated herself on not suggesting that her son only wear socks until he was with his father for Christmas. Their divorce wasn't one of petty squabbles or game playing, as tempting as it was at times. That had been one of her rules when they'd decided to break up. They had to remain kind to one another, thoughtful and friendly, even when they really didn't want to. Even when they were hurting. It was a year since the divorce had come through and, while the pain was still somewhat there, the kindness had become a habit.

'We're going to be late!' shouted Emma from the front door.

Wendy exhaled in a whistle through her teeth. If she had a pound coin for every time her twelve-year-old shouted through the house she could quit her job. That thought caught her by surprise.

'Mum? Are you okay?'

Wendy blinked and found herself frozen, bag half zipped up. She shook herself awake.

'Yes. Yes. Your bag is almost packed, so I'll put it under your bed for now. Okay? Don't take anything out of it but you can add anything you want to take to your dad's. Yeah? Got your socks on?'

Oliver wiggled his socked toes at her.

'Good. Shoes. Quickly now or we'll be late and Emma'll shout at you.'

Oliver pulled a face and ran off to find his shoes. Wendy took a final glance around her son's bedroom and then closed the door, following him down the stairs.

Emma was waiting by the front door dressed in her school uniform, her soft brown hair, inherited from Wendy, tied back in a high ponytail. Wendy hesitated on the stairs long enough to think for the umpteenth time just how much her daughter took after her. Sometimes she wasn't sure that was such a good thing but when it came to school, it was wonderful. As long as Emma stayed on track and wasn't dissuaded by hormones, she would likely follow in her mother's career footsteps too.

For the first time upon having that thought, Wendy frowned. Her hand went to her stomach as it churned.

'Mum?'

Wendy looked up at her daughter.

'Yes. I know, we're going to be late. Come on, Olly!'

Wendy slipped on her trainers, grabbed her bag and car keys, scooped an arm behind Oliver to hurry him out of the house and then locked the door behind them all. Once in the car, Wendy began the drive to the primary school first. In the back, Oliver stared out of the window while in the front passenger seat, Emma studied her phone. Radio turned up, Wendy tuned out.

She would drop the kids off at school then make her way to the car park. She'd stand on the Tube into central London, grabbing a coffee on the way, and reach the office with time to spare. Just like always. She had a few pieces of work to do and some emails to send before she met with James. It would be good to go into the meeting with a clear head.

As far as she was concerned, most of the work was already done. So she could just approve the plans already in place, tell James to put them into action and then get back to her proper job. Except, of course, if the plans were bad because now that would reflect poorly on her. Or if the plans were incomplete. Or if James couldn't put them into action. Or—

'Mum?'

'Hmm?' Wendy pulled over near the primary school.

'Can I go round Stevie's tonight?' Emma asked, exasperated. How many times had she asked while Wendy wasn't listening? No, she was already acting like a teenager, she'd probably only asked the once. The whine in Emma's voice was becoming a permanent thing, something she was learning from Stevie, Wendy suspected. That girl had started whining at the age of eight when her sister had entered her teens. It was enough to give Wendy an eye twitch.

'Do Stevie's parents know?'

She could feel her daughter rolling her eyes.

'Yes. Otherwise she wouldn't have asked.'

Wendy sighed.

'Home by six,' she told her and then held up a hand to silence the protests before they could leave Emma's mouth. 'You have homework to do, school tomorrow and you need to finish packing for going to your dad's.'

'I've still got a week to do that,' said Emma.

'Yes but remember last time? You ended up wearing that top you wanted to take and it was right at the bottom of the washing basket? We don't want that happening again.'

When Emma didn't respond, Wendy risked a glance from the corner of her eye. Her daughter's lips were twisted in an angry pout. Wendy forced away a smile. Emma wanted to argue but there was no logical argument to make, and her daughter was nothing if not logical in her arguments.

'Are you going straight from school?' she asked, only to break the silence.

'Yeah.'

'Okay. Message me.'

'Yes, Mum.'

Wendy ignored the tone. It was only there because Emma was angry she'd lost the argument. She checked Oliver in her rear view mirror.

'You don't have any invites for after school, do you Olly?'

'Nope.'

'Okay.' It might have been nice to not have to worry about getting home so early for them, it would have given her some breathing space. But she'd learnt long ago that after school friend visits couldn't be forced. She got Oliver out of the car, kissed him on the cheek and watched him walk into the playground and into school, waving when she thought he might look back. He didn't. Sighing, she got back in the car. The radio played Christmas music as she drove to the secondary school. It was so close to Christmas. Wendy just had to push through this last unexpected hurdle. Emma climbed out of the car after a brief hug, where her friends wouldn't see, and Wendy was alone. She turned up the radio and started singing along, as loud as she could, until her throat ached and she reached the car park.

Wendy strode into the office bang on time. She settled herself, making a fresh coffee, and checked through her emails. Something – although she couldn't for the life of her say what it was – made her look up just as James walked through the office and past her desk. He was looking down at his phone, coffee in his hand, and a waft of London mixed with cologne came off him as he passed. Wendy stayed looking at him, waiting for his eyes to meet hers so she could tell him they'd talk later, but he didn't look up. He walked past and away, disappearing into a different part of the office. Wendy blinked, her hand finding her stomach. It had to be anxiety about the stupid Christmas fair, she thought. She went to pick up her coffee but thought better of it and sipped at her water in an attempt to calm the fluttering.

'They won't let me have my tinsel.'

Wendy jumped and peered up at the woman next to her.

'What do you mean, they won't let you?'

Kit, a petite, brown-haired woman who looked seventeen but was forty-six (Wendy had been at her last birthday party and had pried the number from Kit after too many gin and tonics), did a flounce as she sat in her chair at the desk beside Wendy.

'Apparently it's distasteful and a fire hazard. Well, it wasn't distasteful and a fire hazard last year. Do you think it's distasteful?'

Wendy studied her friend. They'd met on Kit's first day at the firm when Graham had seated her next to Wendy and told Wendy to show her the ropes. The ropes, on that day, had involved a lengthy tour of the best local restaurant for lunch where the two had discovered a passion for Christmas in common, among other things.

'That depends. What colour was it going to be this year?'

'Silver.'

'That sounds very tasteful. It is a fire hazard, though. And they're hotter on that this year.'

Kit exhaled sharply.

'Health and safety gone mad.'

Wendy slowly turned to look at her friend. Kit grinned and together they whispered under their breath, 'Elf and safety,' before erupting into giggles.

Wendy pulled herself together, sipping at her coffee.

'What did Graham want yesterday?' Kit asked.

'Oh, Sue's gone off sick so I'm to finish organising the Christmas fair.'

This time Kit turned slowly to look at Wendy.

'What? You? Why? How?' She gestured at Wendy's desk and the piles of electronic work that were symbolically stacked upon it.

Wendy leaned over the gap between them so she could lower her voice.

'Not a clue. But they're making the decision about who becomes partner afterwards.'

Kit's eyes widened as the realisation hit her.

'So, you'll only make partner if you can pull off the Christmas fair?' she hissed, shaking her head as Wendy shrugged. 'That's not legal.'

'That's why it's not official.' Wendy sat back. 'I'm guessing. I mean. Maybe I got the wrong end of the stick.' She held up her hands to proclaim innocence.

Kit studied her for a moment.

'What're you going to do?'

Wendy sighed. That was the big question. The one she'd been avoiding all evening. The one she daren't ask herself. She shrugged.

'Get on with it, I guess.'

Kit emitted a soft growl.

'It isn't right. Who's taken over from Sue while she's off? Why can't her team handle it?'

'Look, I'm sure I'm blowing it all out of proportion. Graham says Sue has already organised the thing. I just need to see it through and I'll have the guy who was assisting Sue to help. I'm sure it'll be fine.'

Kit didn't look as sure as Wendy sounded.

'What guy?'

'James something-or-other. One of our juniors.'

Kit's brow furrowed as she tried to place the name.

'Is he cute?'

Wendy shot her a warning look. Kit shrugged.

'Just saying. Something good could come from all this.'

'Yeah, like me being promoted.'

'Oh, I meant before that. It is Christmas, after all.' Kit gave a dirty laugh that Wendy could never resist. She smiled to herself.

'Doesn't your brother's girlfriend organise Christmas events? Maybe she could help,' Kit suggested after a moment of silence as they went through their inboxes.

'Yup. Eve. She's now his wife and they're currently on honeymoon.'

'In December?'

'They were going to have a Christmas wedding but they've started a tradition of holding a Christmas ghost tour in their house in my father's memory. He loved holding ghost tours there and Eve always organised them. They now do a ghost tour before Christmas and a Christmas fair. The fair was at the beginning of the month this year, then they got married, and they'll be home in time for the Christmas ghost tour.'

'Cor. She sounds as married to her job as you

are.'

Wendy didn't respond to that. Her gaze drifted down from her computer screen to a photo of her children, wedged between her pen pot and coaster.

'She loves Christmas,' she murmured eventually.

'Is that your whole family, then? A load of Christmas lovers?' Kit asked, tapping away at her keyboard.

Wendy smiled.

'My older brother's with a professional baker,' she said. 'Beth makes a mean gingerbread man.'

Kit laughed.

'And yet you never bring anything into the office?'

'I meant to last year, but I ate it all instead.'

The two women glanced at one another before giggling quietly. They were interrupted by Kit's phone ringing.

Wendy turned back to her work. Her emails were organised. Sure, there were a couple of calls to make but they could wait. She wondered if James was available now. She typed out a quick message to him and hit send. A reply popped up as she sipped her coffee. He was ready when she was.

3

Wendy exhaled slowly as she wandered over to the meeting room she'd booked for her and James. Her laptop was under one arm and her free hand held a full cup of coffee. He was already in there waiting for her. When she saw him through the glass wall, she slowed. His head was down as he studied his phone. Was he checking social media? His laptop was in front of him so he wasn't looking at emails. Perhaps his wife had messaged him. Or his girlfriend. Or boyfriend, or husband... Wendy mentally shook herself. What did it matter if a partner had messaged him? His shirt sleeves were down this morning but her eyes were still drawn to his arms and his fingers, sliding over the screen of his phone.

'Crying out loud,' Wendy muttered to herself, silently banishing any butterflies that were threatening to fall into her stomach. She pushed open the door and almost dropped her laptop on the large table in the centre of the small room.

'Good morning,' she said a little too briskly.

'Morning.' He looked up, placing his phone screen down on the table.

Wendy arranged herself, opening her laptop and sipping her coffee. He'd brought a glass of water, she noticed, which sat untouched.

'Everything okay?' she asked as her laptop woke up. James nodded, studying his own laptop screen as he tapped some keys.

'How did you get roped into helping Sue organise this, then?' Wendy asked, unwittingly tapping her foot as the unnecessary nervous butterflies were pushed from her stomach and into her toes.

A small smile flittered across James's face but he kept his eyes on his screen.

'I volunteered. For some reason I thought it would look good.'

Wendy smiled to herself.

'Apparently it does look good,' she murmured.

James looked up at that.

'Does it?'

She lifted her gaze automatically and locked eyes with him. His were a deep brown, as dark as the hair on his arms, and then the butterflies were out of her toes and back in her stomach, tapping their wings against her insides.

'That's why I'm here,' she said weakly.

He gave her a curious look and Wendy cleared her throat.

'So, the fair is in a week. I imagine Sue has everything sorted by now?'

James laughed. It echoed around the minimalist room, making Wendy jump.

'She should have done but nope.'

Nope. Wendy blinked.

'What do you mean, nope?'

James's shoulders sagged and he turned his laptop so the screen faced her.

'This is the folder we shared with everything in it. This is a list of all her ideas. This is a spreadsheet of everything that needs doing.' He opened the document. 'See this column? This is the completed column.'

There was a long list of things to be done but the completed column was gut-wrenchingly empty. Wendy pulled her gaze from the empty spreadsheet column to the one filled with the to do list.

Book stallholders.

Contact charities.

Create layout and map.

Organise music.

Organise food.

She looked up at James, eyes wide.

'Tell me most of this is done and she just forgot to tick it off,' she murmured in a hushed voice, terrified of the answer.

James's eyes softened and he slowly shook his head.

'But the stallholders are booked. Right?'

'Some are,' said James. 'But not enough. Maybe

three?'

'Three! Okay. But the charities are sorted, right?'

'Oh, yes. Sort of.'

'Sort of?'

'Well, Marketing sorted most of it and I think Sue had some initial chats. We have our main charity but it was originally decided we'd work with three. We could change that, though, I guess.'

Wendy sighed. The space between her eyes twinged with the makings of a headache.

'How has this happened?' she murmured, her thoughts spinning. 'No, okay, if we have to do this right then we'll need the three charities.' She refrained from swearing.

James sat back in thought.

'Two small charities. What's your favourite one?' Wendy asked.

'A local one that helps homeless people with their pets,' said James.

Wendy smiled, glancing up at him.

'Mine's a homeless charity too but focusing on the people. Great, we'll approach them.' Wendy scribbled down the note. 'You contact yours, I'll contact mine. Tell them the proceeds will be split into thirds. Is that what Sue had planned?'

'Think so,' said James, making a note for himself.

Wendy nodded. One thing down, many more to go. Arguably, choosing charities was the easy part. She sighed, staring at the to do list. What was next?

Her chest was tightening with each breath. How was she going to pull this off? They had one week, nothing was planned, and she was a solicitor not an event organiser. Even an event organiser couldn't pull this one off.

'At least the venue's booked,' she murmured.

The silence made her look up at James. He was cringing.

'That's also a nope.'

'What?' Wendy screeched. 'There's no venue? There's no venue.' She sat back as it sank in. 'How the hell are we going to do this in a week without a venue? Everywhere'll be booked. Why hadn't Sue done anything? Why hadn't she at least booked a venue?'

'She hadn't been feeling well for a while,' James told her. 'She reckons she was burned out. I reckon she... Well, that's not important.'

'No, go on.' Wendy leaned forward so they could lower their voices. 'You reckon...' she urged.

James glanced around as if there might be a spy sitting in the corner of the meeting room and then leaned closer, whispering, 'I reckon she's not ill. I reckon she's bailed because she didn't book a venue.'

'But why?' Wendy asked. 'What were you doing through all this? Couldn't you have booked a venue for her?'

James stiffened and sighed, shoulders heaving.

'I tried, believe me. I kept offering to do things. I

told her so many times I was happy to book anything and everything and she kept saying, over and over, no, she had it under control. Until one day I told her that it was okay if she was struggling or whatever, that's what I'm here for, to help. I said I'd go book a venue that minute and she pretty much screamed at me not to. I have no idea what was going on with her, but I doubt she's really ill. And I wanted to help. I'll do whatever you want me to, but c'mon. I'm the new guy here. I've never done this before. I didn't want to overstep my bounds and suddenly this woman is screaming at me not to do anything. So I didn't.' James slumped back in his chair.

Wendy watched, her foot tapping faster against the floor.

'I'm sorry she shouted at you. That's not on at all.' What had Sue been playing at? Wendy didn't like to think badly of the woman. She'd organised the Christmas fair before, although Wendy couldn't remember how good it had been. Had she even attended? Maybe Sue was just overworked, over-burdened, burned out.

Wendy stifled something of a hysterical laugh, thinking of the stacks of cases, the clients who had burst into tears during their meetings, the running from work to school to home, the worry, the sleepless nights wondering what she'd forgotten. Running a hand over her face, Wendy shook her head.

'This is insane. I can't do this.' She hadn't meant to say that last bit out loud but there it was, hanging over the table between them. She daren't look up at James. That was certainly not something a senior associate was supposed to say in front of a junior.

He didn't say anything. Why wasn't he saying anything?

She risked a glance at him. He was staring down at the table, lips pursed, possibly thinking through his options. That's what she should have been doing.

'I'll talk to Graham,' she murmured after a moment. There were only two options: get on with it or talk to Graham. Her first move was obvious. 'Can you give me access to that to do list?'

James nodded, pulling his laptop closer. Wendy moved to stand.

'I'll let you know what happens.'

'What about the charities?' James asked, following her.

'If we don't hold the fair, I'm sure the firm can still donate,' said Wendy, heading for the door. She had to catch Graham quickly and hope that he was in a good mood. Surely he'd see the sense of cancelling the fair. He had to.

'Thanks,' she added as she left James by his desk.

There was a part of her desperate to turn around as she walked away, to give him a reassuring smile perhaps, which was ridiculous.

'Focus,' she muttered as she spotted Graham

heading into his office with a fresh cup of coffee. 'Graham!' she called, breaking into a light mince of a jog which was arguably no faster than the walk she'd been doing. It did the trick, though. He hesitated to look at her, his brow creasing in tired curiosity.

'Everything all right?' he asked as she reached him.

'Do you have a moment? I need to talk to you,' she said, heaving her laptop under her arm and hoping she'd be able to find the spreadsheet easily.

Graham gestured for her to enter his office and he closed the door behind them. Wendy took the chair opposite his desk and opened her laptop. An email from James pinged through with a link to the spreadsheet. She exhaled in a rush.

'What's this about, Wendy?' Graham sat in his chair, sipping his coffee.

'I just met with James about the Christmas fair,' said Wendy, head down, eyes still on the screen as she pulled up the document. 'He showed me how much Sue has done so far.'

'Hmm?'

Wendy lifted her laptop and turned it, placing it on the desk so Graham could see the to do list with nothing completed.

'She's done nothing, Graham. Nothing's done. Nothing's ready. There's not even a venue booked. What the hell was she doing in all that time? James kept trying to organise it for her and she kept telling him no until she shouted at him. She shouted at him, Graham. He did everything he could and she did nothing. Now we have one week to pull off this huge event. It's not possible.'

There was a silence as Wendy waited, heart pounding. Graham's eyes flicked over the screen. Then he leaned forward and pulled Wendy's laptop closer, working his way through the document, his features dropping until finally he heaved a deep sigh.

He sat back in his chair, staring through Wendy, biting his lip in thought, tapping his fingers against the desk. She watched and waited, her mouth dry.

'Last year you mentioned you had invested in your sister's business,' Graham said quietly.

Wendy's heart fluttered. That wasn't the reaction she'd been expecting.

'Well, yes, my sister-in-law, but—'

'An event business, isn't it?'

'Weddings. But—'

'An event is an event, isn't it? Is this the same sister who runs the events at your old home?'

Wendy closed her eyes and took a deep breath.

'Yes, it is. She's a wedding planner but she also runs a Christmas ghost tour and fair at the Manor.'

'A Christmas fair?' Graham's eyes lit up.

'She's on her honeymoon, Graham,' said Wendy quickly. 'She can't help. We've got one week and even she, a professional event planner, would struggle with this. I am not contacting her on her

225

honeymoon. She hasn't had a holiday all year because she's been working so hard on her business. I am not asking for her help. She has enough to do.' Wendy gritted her teeth for a moment. 'As do I. I have worked damn hard this year – no, this decade, Graham. I have put everything into this job, everything. I will not be judged for a promotion based on a Christmas fair that the original organiser couldn't be arsed to work on, for whatever reason. This isn't my job. I'm a solicitor and I'm a damn good one. One of your best. Which is why I deserve to be made partner, whether or not this fair goes ahead. Which, by the way, I don't think it should. Cancel the fair. Make a donation to the charities and be done with it.' Wendy sat back, breathing hard, and crossed her arms over her chest to signal the end of the matter.

Graham watched her, his jawline tense.

'You are one of our best, Wendy,' he said steadily. 'You have certainly worked hard since you started here. We have no reason to doubt your skills or your work ethic.'

Something inside Wendy shifted. There was a sudden urge to vomit.

'But we cannot and will not have a year without a Christmas fair. This firm has been holding a charitable Christmas fair for thirty years, Wendy. That tradition is ours and if you become partner, it will become your tradition. If you want to be partner, it is your tradition. Right now. Do you want thirty years of tradition to grind to a halt because of you?'

Wendy blinked, her fingertips tingling as she leaned forward.

'Because of you,' she said quietly. 'Because you gave this job to Sue and then didn't check what she was doing.'

Graham's eyes narrowed.

'She volunteered. And she will be dealt with when she returns. We now have one week to pull off a Christmas fair otherwise I'll be in trouble and so will you. Do you understand?' His hands were trembling as he closed her laptop and pushed it back to her. 'Both of us will suffer here.'

'Because you're going to take me down with you,' Wendy murmured, tears springing hot into her eyes.

'Or you could save us both,' Graham told her. 'I'll take your cases from you. You have one week, yes, but you'll have nothing else to do and James will help you. I'll find others to help if you need them, just say. We need this Christmas fair to happen, Wendy, and we need it to be good.'

There wasn't much else to say, there wasn't much else to do. Wendy left Graham's office fighting back the tears, hiding her trembling fingers. She walked calmly to the toilets where she let the tears fall silently, her body convulsing as the shock of the meeting worked its way through her. Crying done, body calming, she blew her nose, tidied her make-up and ventured back out into the office. She messaged James – she couldn't cope with facing him just yet – and then she hid in a back office with her laptop and a notebook trying to work out how they were going to pull this off with one week to go, until she had to leave to pick her children up from school.

4

That evening, Wendy sat at her dining table with her laptop and a glass of wine. Her son was in the living room curled up on the sofa in his pyjamas watching online videos. Emma was in her bedroom listening to music that Wendy had asked to be turned down twice already. Wendy was staring at Sue's to do list, surrounded by the notes she'd made that day. She'd researched event planning and just what people expected at Christmas fairs. She'd tried to remember the firm's previous fairs but her memory of them was hazy. The only vivid memories she had was when Oliver had been small, pulling her this way and that at each bright colour and twinkling light while her husband had kept hold of Emma's hand. Her husband had smiled at her, wrapping a warm arm around her waist and suggested they grab something to eat before they headed home. She couldn't for the life of her remember any part of the fair in detail, at least nothing that was useful. There had been food.

There had been bright colours and twinkling lights.

James had sent Wendy the meagre list of contacts Sue had graced him with. Wendy had spent the afternoon calling them to find that everyone was booked. She knew that she needed a venue, which tended to be different each year. She needed decorations and stallholders, she needed food and drink, and maybe entertainment. The thing was, all of that was already on the to do list. She hadn't learned anything new. The day had been a waste.

Wendy stared at her blank phone, sipped her wine and then sighed. Picking up the phone, she checked on Oliver, listened out for Emma and, satisfied both children were safe and doing what they should be doing, she called a friend.

'Help,' she said after she'd finished explaining the situation.

There was a pause at the other end of the line.

'Are you sure you want my help?' asked Beth. 'Sounds to me like you should tell your boss where to stick it.'

'Ten years, Beth. Just over ten years I've been working my arse off at this firm and I'm so close. I'm a week away from making partner and all I have to do is put together a Christmas fair.'

'In a week. Less than a week, actually,' Beth pointed out. 'It's on the Friday, right? There's really not a lot of time.'

'Which is why I'm asking you for help. I didn't want to bother Eve on her honeymoon. I thought maybe you'd have some of her contacts?'

Beth sighed down the phone.

'I don't. But I'll figure it out. I'll help but I'm not happy about this and I'll tell you why. I don't mind helping you put on an event at short notice, especially if it's something you really want. But I'm not happy about you being used like this. You know what my experience of this is? You do all the work, you put together the best event possible and you still don't get the promotion. What're you going to do if that happens?'

Wendy clenched her eyes shut. That didn't bear thinking about.

'Trying not to think about that,' she said quietly.

'Is she in trouble?' Something about the deep voice of Wendy's big brother in the background made her insides relax a little.

'Tell you later,' Beth told him. 'I'm in London right now with Glen,' she continued to Wendy. 'I'll see what I can pull together and I'll meet you tomorrow, yeah? Give me a time and place.'

Tears pricked Wendy's eyes. Tears filled with relief instead of the shock of her earlier outburst.

'Thank you so much. I owe you. Big time.'

'Of course you don't. You're family. But if you don't get this promotion, I'm going to punch your boss in his face.'

Wendy laughed. They spoke a little more and then Beth handed the phone to Wendy's brother.

'Why are we punching your boss in the face?'

Glen asked.

'Beth will explain, I'm sure,' said Wendy.

'You okay? You sound wobbly.'

'I... Yeah, I'm fine,' said Wendy, her stomach turning as she lied. She wasn't fine. Placing a hand on her belly, she drifted from the conversation. The last time she'd felt this way was the day she'd asked her husband for a divorce.

'Nice to have two weeks off for once. So we're spending Christmas with Jeff and Eve. Are you coming?'

'I am,' said Wendy. 'The kids are going to their dad's so...' Wendy drifted off as an idea wedged itself into her thoughts.

'Okay. We'll miss them.'

'Yeah.'

'Rob's coming. We gave him the choice this year and he said he wanted to go to the Manor. Pretty sure it's just so he can eat everything Beth bakes.'

'That's nice. I feel like I haven't seen Rob in ages.' It had been a year since Wendy had seen her nephew. She imagined he'd grown another few inches, he'd be a full adult now. She really needed to make more time for family. Her gaze drifted through the doors to the living room where she could still make out the sound of the video Oliver was watching.

They said their goodbyes and Wendy promised to message Beth of a place to meet the following morning. Once they'd hung up, Wendy called her ex-husband and crossed her toes, hidden in their cosy socks, that he'd agree to have the children a week early.

Beth met Wendy by the Tube station for a quick coffee.

'Feels like a while,' Beth said. 'How are you?'

Wendy's shoulders sank down. She hadn't even realised they were basically in her ears.

'Stressed,' she said with a small laugh.

Beth looked on with concern.

'Glen told me the other day how much you loved Christmas when you were a kid. Even at university, you'd always come home dressed in special Christmas outfits.' Beth smiled. 'Did you come home dressed as a reindeer once? Please tell me that's true.'

Wendy nearly spat out her coffee.

'Oh. I did. I'd forgotten about that.' She grinned. 'Not dressed as an actual reindeer. I had a reindeer patterned dress on but I did walk into the house wearing a pair of these soft antlers. I remember Dad and Jeff laughing. Glen and Mum thought I was mad.' Her grin softened at the memory. 'Glen always was more like Mum.'

Beth cocked her head to the side, studying her.

'Who are you most like?'

Wendy frowned.

'People used to say I was like Dad. Turning up with antlers was something he'd do.' She looked up into Beth's eyes. 'I don't know who I'm like anymore,' she said quietly.

'You're like you,' Beth told her, putting a reassuring hand on hers. 'Don't shout at me but I spoke to Eve.'

'You didn't have to do that,' said Wendy immediately, pulling away.

'Yes I did. You want this fair to go well and the only person with the ability to pull something like this off in a week is Eve. You need her contacts if nothing else. She emailed everything over to me, I've forwarded it to you.'

Wendy hesitated. She really hadn't wanted to disturb her new sister-in-law. Beth had been friends with Eve since they were students and now it looked like Beth was on her way to becoming Wendy's other sister-in-law. They'd become one big family fast, maybe she shouldn't feel so guilty.

'Thank you,' she said. 'So much. Thank you. I really appreciate it. You have no idea how much.'

Beth smiled and drained her coffee.

'No, I do. You forget that I used to work in London, all high and mighty with lots of figures in my salary. I remember the pressure, the stress. What I want you to remember, or to know, is that there are other ways. I mean, look at me. I left all that pressure and stress behind and now I run a successful bakery, I'm working with my best friends, helping with the catering at events and I'm with an incredible man who I love.'

'I won't tell my brother,' said Wendy without

missing a beat. They smiled at one another.

'There's another life, Wendy. If you want it. That's all I'm saying. And that I'm here if you need me. And Eve. We both are.' Beth stood and got ready to leave. 'We're just at the end of the phone, whenever.'

The women hugged and went their separate ways. Beth headed back to Glen and a planned day of wandering around festively decorated tourist attractions in the city. Wendy walked to the office where she found James waiting for her.

'We need a venue,' he told her after she explained where she'd been. Had he slept? His hair suggested he hadn't. That pang of guilt resurfaced in Wendy.

'My sister's given me a list of her venue contacts. You take half, I'll take the other. Let's see if anyone has availability.'

The day moved quickly, the weak December sun moving across the office. Slowly, as the evening approached, the office began to empty.

'Don't you need to go get your kids?' James asked after an hour of silence. They'd found empty desks so they could work close to one another, listening as they each called venues to ask about availability.

'They've gone to their dad's early. They were meant to go at the end of the week, for Christmas.'

'Oh,' said James. 'I'm sorry. That this is taking you away from your kids.'

Wendy shrugged uncomfortably.

'It'll be worth it in the end. And it's fine. A week away from them while I'm working isn't a problem. It's Christmas without them that I'm not looking forward to.'

There was a long pause as Wendy stared out of the window, over the city.

'You should go home,' she told James. 'It's getting late. And your kids are probably waiting for you.'

'I hope not,' James laughed. Wendy met his gaze. 'I don't have kids,' he explained. 'In fact, the only thing waiting for me at home is an annoying housemate and his loud girlfriend. Trust me, I'd rather be working.'

Wendy found herself studying James.

'We'll get more done if we work through the evening,' she murmured.

He nodded, eyes back on his screen.

'But only if we stay fuelled. I'll go order us some pizza, yeah?' Wendy suggested.

James looked up, his eyes brightening.

'Perfect.' He sat back and rolled his shirt sleeves up. Wendy tried not to notice, never mind stare, as his bare arms were revealed. James undid the top button on his shirt, revealing a hint of dark hair that possibly covered his chest. Wendy blinked and looked away. 'I'll grab some more coffee,' he added, going to stand.

'Yes,' said Wendy, the word coming too fast. 'I'll

go, erm, order that pizza.' She watched him walk away towards the coffee machine. What was going on with her? Her stomach was churning, her heart pounding. She was hungry. It was the hunger and the stress, and maybe too much caffeine. That was all. Finding her phone, she went to order the pizza. Once she had some food inside her and had gotten some work done, everything would settle down.

5

'That's it,' said James, slamming the phone down and grabbing a slice of pizza. 'It's official. There are no venues available next Friday in London. The city is booked solid.'

Wendy groaned, covering her face with her hands and pulling on her hair in frustration before straightening, composing herself. It was just gone half seven and they'd wasted another day trying to find a venue, any venue, that was available on Friday. Wendy crossed her arms on the desk and lay her head on one arm. It would be so easy to go to sleep.

'Why hadn't Sue done anything?' she said. 'Was she angry? Was she trying to get Graham in trouble?'

James finished his slice of pizza and shrugged.

'I don't know. I haven't been here long enough to really understand the politics of this place.'

Wendy studied him until her neck hurt and she was forced to sit up again.

'How long have you been here?' she asked.

'I guess maybe seven or eight months,' said James, leaning back in his chair and stretching his arms above his head. Wendy yanked her gaze from his arms and chest and back to the papers on her desk.

'You're a little older than the juniors we normally get,' she said.

'Yeah. I'm one of those people who gets to their late twenties, gets the promotion they've been working for and realises it's not everything they thought it would be. I think they call it a quarter-life crisis, although I had mine a little late.'

'What were you doing? I mean, what was the promotion?'

James grinned and Wendy faltered. Evening James was different to normal working hours James. He had relaxed now that the office was dark and it was just the two of them. Exhaustion and pizza probably helped. The man was not just attractive, he had the most amazing smile. Wendy swallowed, discovered her mouth was dry and sipped at her lukewarm coffee. She pulled a face at the taste.

'Could do with some beers,' James said quietly, watching her. She nodded.

'We can't drink coffee all night.'

'I'll go to the shop down the road.' James stood, stretching again, reaching for his coat and scarf. 'Do you want anything else?'

'Chocolate,' said Wendy without thinking. Heat rushed to her cheeks. James flashed that smile again.

'Won't be long,' he said, sweeping past the desks and striding out of the office. Wendy watched, biting her lower lip. What was she doing? Sure, it had been a long time since she'd been with a man. The last man in her life had been her husband. She was pretty sure the life of a newly divorced woman was supposed to be filled with new acquaintances and rebound sex, but instead Wendy had focused on her career and her children. There wasn't any time for romance, there wasn't any space left in her head.

There was definitely no time or space for an office romance, that would only cause trouble. Wendy pushed all thoughts of James and his rolled up shirt sleeves out of her head and returned to their still unticked to do list.

'No venue. Only a few stallholders. But we have three charities and three jobs on the line.' She sighed, which quickly turned into a loud groan, echoing around the empty office.

By the time James returned with six bottles of beer and a large bar of milk chocolate, Wendy had kicked off her shoes and was contemplating opening a window to scream out into the darkness of the evening.

'Did a venue magically appear?' James asked, handing her the chocolate and a beer. She took them gratefully.

'Maybe we could hold it here,' said Wendy. 'How much do I owe you?'

James looked around.

'Could we? And don't worry about it. I'm earning more now than I ever have. Let me treat you to emergency beer and chocolate.'

Wendy smiled and took a swig of the beer. The bubbles swam through her body and she exhaled.

'That's good. Thank you. You never did say what you used to do.'

'Tree surgeon,' said James.

Wendy stared at him, forcing back images of him up a tree with a chainsaw.

'You can get promoted in the world of tree surgeons?'

James nodded, gulping down some beer.

'In this case, the owner of the company decided to retire and offered me the job of managing director.'

'Wow. Nice. It was a big company then?'

'Growing all the time.'

'And you turned it down?' Wendy frowned. Why would someone work so hard for that job and then turn it down?

'No, no. I accepted it. Did it for two years and then realised that something was still missing. Spent another year wondering if the thing that was missing was a family, realised that it was the job that was making me miserable. Spent yet another year trying to figure out what to do next and then went to university, part time at first. Decided it wasn't going quick enough, quit the job, became a full time student, moved back in with my mum and stepdad, took a job at a supermarket, worked my arse off and here I am. Bottom of the rung at a solicitors firm in London. Living the dream.' James lifted his bottle of beer in toast to Wendy.

'Are you enjoying it?' she asked.

'I was,' said James, taking a swig from his bottle. 'Until I thought it would be a good idea to volunteer to help organise the firm's Christmas fair.'

Wendy laughed. James grinned, looking down at the bottle in his hand, fiddling with the label.

'It's hard. Being the oldest in the team. Surrounded by people ten years younger than me who have all this energy and all this ambition. It's hard to compete with them. I thought volunteering for the fair would put me ahead. I don't know what I was thinking.'

'No, it was a good idea,' Wendy told him. 'The bosses have noticed you.'

James raised an eyebrow.

'Maybe not for the right reasons.'

'Why? You haven't done anything wrong here, Sue did. And from the sound of it, there's a chance she'll be out of this place by spring. If Graham has anything to do with it. Or maybe she'll hand in her notice and never come back. Either way, it was a good idea to volunteer. You have to do stuff like that at the beginning. When I was a junior I was always volunteering for projects.'

'Did you ever organise a Christmas fair?'

'No.' Wendy smiled to herself. 'But I wish I could have. I would have loved it. Christmas has always been my favourite time of year.'

James's brow creased.

'Really? I hate Christmas.'

Wendy snapped up, staring at James as silence descended on the office. Those three words hung over their heads.

'But, why?' she breathed.

James gave her a curious look, a small lopsided smile twitching at his lips. He shrugged it all away.

'My dad used to get drunk on Christmas Day, my parents would argue and then, to really rub salt in the wound, my fiancé dumped me on Christmas Eve. For a while there, any sort of Christmas music would make me feel sick.'

Wendy sagged back for a moment and then offered him some of the chocolate.

'I'm not surprised,' she said. 'I think that would probably do it for me too.'

James declined the offer, the dark shadow that had passed over his eyes as he spoke lifting as he looked up at her. His eyes were a delicious shade of dark chocolate in this light and in that moment, Wendy became acutely aware of how alone they were in the office.

'So why do you love Christmas?' he asked.

Wendy took a gulp of beer, giving it some thought.

'The opposite reasons, I guess. Except for the fiancé. My husband never cared much about Christmas. It's just another day. That's what he'd always say. But when I was little, my family was all about Christmas.' Wendy smiled as the memories flooded through. 'My dad was the playful sort. In the last few years of his life, he worked with my new sister-in-law to hold Christmas ghost tours at our old family home without telling any of us. I reckon he knew we'd all disapprove. Mum would have disapproved. She's the one who made that house a home. Christmas was always twinkling lights and hot chocolate with marshmallows, incredible food and amazing smells, and always the biggest tree my dad could find that year. We'd all decorate it together.' Wendy chuckled to herself. 'I'd race with my brothers up the stairs to reach the highest branches but it was always Dad's job to put the angel on top. On their first Christmas together, my mum gave him this angel for the tree with this hilarious look on her face. Like she really didn't appreciate having a tree up her skirt. Dad loved her.' Wendy softened. 'My little brother puts her on the top of the tree now. I guess that's the difference. A happy family. Sure, there were arguments, there were five of us. But someone always played peacemaker.' Wendy realised she'd been talking for too long and stopped herself, adding quietly,

'Christmas was always magic.' She looked up to find James staring at her, his eyes soft but his brow creased in question.

'Racing up the stairs to decorate the top of the tree?' he asked. 'What sort of house was this?'

Heat rushed to Wendy's chest and cheeks.

'Erm, an old manor house. It's called the Manor, actually. I grew up in a little town about an hour or so from London.'

'You're from money,' James said gently.

Wendy flinched.

'I guess. That's not to say my parents didn't work damn hard though.'

'Oh, I have no doubt,' said James, his voice softening. 'You've got an incredible work ethic.'

Wendy glanced at him to check if he was joking. There was nothing mocking about the look he was giving her.

'Well, it hardly matters. My parents are gone, the money is mostly gone. Dad passed away two years ago, he left the house to my little brother and I spent my inheritance on my divorce. The rest has gone into a fund for my kids when they get old enough.'

'He left the house to the youngest? That's... different,' said James.

'Hmm. Jeff's an architect. He always took after Dad the most. I think that's why.'

'You weren't happy about it?'

Wendy looked up in surprise. What had she done

to give that away? She gave him a weak smile.

'I had this stupid notion that moving to my old childhood home would fix my marriage.'

It was James's turn to sigh.

'Sorry about your marriage.'

'Sorry about your fiancé. That's horrible. What a bitch to do it on Christmas Eve,' said Wendy without thinking. She snapped her mouth closed but James laughed.

'Yeah, turns out she was sleeping with my friend's brother and she wanted to spend Christmas with him.'

Wendy's eyebrows shot up, her mouth hanging open. James waved her shock away.

'It's fine. It was a while ago.'

There was a comfortable pause as they both looked down at their laptops, trying to remember what they were there for.

'Why did you choose to become a solicitor, after all that?' Wendy asked quietly.

When James didn't answer immediately, she glanced up at him. He was looking up at the ceiling, lifting his beer to his lips. After he'd swallowed his mouthful, he flashed a smile at her.

'I wanted to help people. How cheesy is that?'

'Not at all,' said Wendy. 'It's the only good reason to get into it. It's why I got into it. Well, that and the money.'

They stared at one another for a moment and then both burst out laughing.

'Oh, what're we gonna do about this stupid venue?' James groaned, sitting up properly and nudging his laptop. 'Can we do it here? How about an online fair?'

Wendy pulled a face. The beer had seeped into her mind, thoughts crashing into one another.

'Hang on,' she said, pulling out her phone. James watched, leaning forward as if that would help him see what she was typing. 'There.' She hit send and then stared at her phone, waiting for those little dots that suggested Eve was messaging her back.

'What's there? What have you done?' asked James, straining to see.

'Messaged my sister-in-law. She's on her honeymoon but needs must. Now that she's married my little brother, the Manor is also hers. We run a wedding planning business together.' Wendy hiccupped and smacked a hand over her mouth. James gave her an amused grin. 'That's a lie,' she said, removing her hand. 'I'm a silent partner in her events business. Jeff will say no if I ask him, but he can't say no to her. Because he's so in love, blah, blah, blah.'

James raised an eyebrow.

'Don't tell me divorce has made you cynical?'

Wendy laughed.

'Of course it has. Didn't your experience make you cynical?'

James nodded.

'Yeah but if the last few years have taught me anything, it's that love matters. Sex without love is boring.' He smacked his hand over his mouth then, eyes wide, cheeks blushing. Wendy laughed.

'Don't worry,' she told him. 'I won't think any less of you for that.'

'No more drinking when working,' said James.

They clinked their beers together and Wendy's phone beeped.

'Is that your sister?'

Wendy opened the message, her heart pounding, stomach turning. What was she doing?

She read the message and jumped to her feet, pounding the air with her fist and hollering into the dark, empty building. James watched.

'Is that a yes?'

'James. We are officially using the Manor as the venue for this year's Christmas fair. Do you know what that means?' Wendy held out a hand and James took it as a sign to stand up.

'What does it mean?'

'It means that this Christmas fair is going to be the best one this firm has ever held.'

They clinked their beers together again and James drained his as Wendy messaged Eve back.

6

'What happened after that?'

Wendy sat in Beth's bakery on the high street of the town she grew up in. The windows were steamed up around stickers of snowflakes, soft Christmas music was playing and there was the ever present smell of coffee and sweet treats in the air. Wendy had her elbows on the table in the window of the café, her head in her hands. She groaned loudly.

'Nothing. I think,' she said, her words muffled.

'And you've been working with him since? I mean, you've seen him since, right?' came Beth's voice. Wendy did a strange nod, still not removing her face from her hands.

'So, what's the problem?'

The problem was that the evening alone with James in the office had broken something. There was now something unspoken between them. Words desperate to be said. The following morning, Wendy had walked into the office with a pounding headache and little recollection of getting home.

She'd drunk too much coffee and when faced with James, had skipped over the awkward silence he'd introduced and become the most professional solicitor she could be.

With the Manor booked as the venue and Eve eager to help, even from abroad, the fair had pretty much organised itself. Eve had built up such goodwill over the years that the stallholders from the Manor's earlier fair were happy to return at such short notice.

'You like him, don't you,' said Beth, sitting back with a smile like a proud detective who had just solved a case.

Wendy's stomach did a small panicked flutter.

'He's a nice guy,' she tried.

'No. No. I mean you like him. The same way I like your brother.'

'Don't,' Wendy warned.

'You want to kiss him. And sleep next to him. And—'

'Don't!'

Beth beamed at her, the grin slowly fading as Wendy didn't smile back.

'Seriously, what's the problem? He sounds great. And like maybe he feels the same way. You're allowed to be attracted to someone, you know. You're allowed to indulge yourself. Have sex, be reckless, fall in love, have some fun. Whatever you want.'

Wendy's heart pounded, her head spinning.

'I can't.'

'Why not?'

'Because I'm a mother and a solicitor and I want to make partner,' Wendy blurted.

Beth blinked.

'And mothers can't fall in love? Solicitors can't have any fun?'

Wendy struggled, shifting in her chair. Beth leaned across the table and asked in a quiet voice, 'What happens after you make partner? What then?'

Wendy stopped. Holding her breath, she thought furiously. What would happen then?

'Well,' she started slowly. 'I'll be earning more.'

'Yeah. So?' Beth said.

'So, I don't have to worry anymore.'

'You're worrying about money?' Beth asked.

There was the tinkle of the bell over the door and then, 'Why are you worried about money? Do you need help?'

Wendy smiled, turning to look up at her big brother as he entered the café with a concerned frown. Beth smiled and stood, going up on tiptoe to kiss Glen's lips before asking if he wanted a coffee. He nodded and pulled a chair up to their table.

'No. No, I'm not worried about money,' Wendy told them both.

'So is making partner really that important?' Beth asked from the coffee machine.

'What? She's been talking about running a law

firm since we were little,' said Glen.

'Do partners actually run the firm?' Beth reappeared with a coffee for Glen and a plate of three freshly baked mince pies. Glen immediately took one and bit into it. He'd always been bigger than their dad and Jeff, he'd always had broader shoulders and thicker muscles. As he'd aged, he started to put weight on but he'd definitely put more on since he and Beth had gotten together. He said eating delicious things was one of the benefits of somehow convincing Beth to fall in love with him.

'That's exactly what it means,' said Wendy.

'So you can't just leave and start your own law firm? The same way I left my job and started a bakery?'

'You could do that,' said Glen before finishing off the mince pie.

'Yeah, but...' Wendy drifted off. She frowned. There were arguments against starting her own law firm, it was just that in that moment, she couldn't think of them.

'That way you could get together with this James guy and it wouldn't matter that you work together or you're more senior than him or that you'd become his boss,' said Beth. 'Because that's the problem, right?'

Wendy stared at her.

'Is it?' She glanced at Glen who shrugged, swallowing his mouthful.

'Who's James?' he asked.

Wendy turned her attention back to Beth.

'That's not the problem,' she said, although as the words came out something inside her recoiled.

'Then what is?' Beth asked.

A silence descended upon the table as Wendy searched for a reply. Eventually, she shook her head.

'I'm not attracted to him. There is no problem. There.' Wendy took her mince pie and bit defiantly into it. The pastry melted in her mouth and she let out a moan without thinking. Glen smiled knowingly. 'So, the Christmas fair,' Wendy continued as Beth opened her mouth to protest. 'I have to go to the Manor later to start setting everything up. I don't suppose you can help?'

'Of course,' said Beth. She grinned. 'Eve messaged me this morning to make sure I'm helping you. I think she's actually annoyed that she's missing it.'

'She'll be annoyed she's missing out on her honeymoon at this rate,' Wendy murmured.

'I can help too,' said Glen. 'What do we need to do?'

'Great. Thanks. You can check the lights are all still up and set up the sound system with James while Beth helps me with the stalls, maybe?' Wendy didn't know. She was making this up as she went along, but there was only so much help she could ask from Eve.

'Oh. James will be there?' Beth grinned again, taking her mince pie and breaking it in half.

'Yes and I need both of you to behave. Please. Please don't say anything,' Wendy begged.

Beth gave her a look.

'Of course we won't. Will we,' she said to Glen.

'About what?' Glen asked, his eyes full of sincerity.

'See. No need to worry.' Beth handed half of her mince pie to Glen who blew her a kiss before popping it into his mouth.

'Have you been enjoying this at all?' Glen asked as he chewed. 'You used to love Christmas. I don't mind telling you now, it used to really annoy me when you married and suddenly couldn't do Christmas your way anymore.'

Wendy looked up at her brother.

'I didn't think anyone noticed,' she said quietly. 'I don't think I even noticed until recently.'

Glen frowned and shook his head, swallowing his mouthful.

'We noticed. It was when you were pregnant with Emma and suddenly you were going to a restaurant for Christmas dinner with your in-laws. But you love to cook.'

'I was really sick during that pregnancy,' Wendy murmured, her stomach turning at the memory.

'You always said you were going to call your daughter Holly, or Tinkerbell – remember? It was a bit of a shock when you introduced her as Emma.

Then after that you weren't allowed all the decorations. Remember? Just a tree and nothing else.'

Wendy's breath caught, her eyes burning.

'You wouldn't have put up with that when we were kids,' Glen continued. He grinned at a memory. 'Remember that dress you had? The red one with the white fluffy bits?'

'White fluffy bits?' asked Beth.

'The trim,' Wendy told her. 'Like a Santa Claus dress.'

'Oh, I can see you in something like that,' said Beth. 'That would be very you.'

'It was,' Glen agreed. He studied his sister. 'You're running a Christmas fair to get the promotion you deserve,' he told her. 'It's not right, pretty sure it's not legal, and you've worked so hard on it. The least you can do is enjoy it.'

'See? What was I saying?' said Beth, finishing her mince pie. 'It's time you started having fun again. You're free, you're single, you can be you.' Beth brushed the crumbs from her fingers and looked Wendy in the eye. 'Get back to being you.'

Wendy's gaze moved from Beth and her brother, down to the table and then to her coffee. They weren't wrong. Something inside her had shifted as they'd spoken. Her lips twitched as she remembered that Christmas dress she'd had as a child. It had been her favourite.

Her phone vibrated against the table as it silently rang. Wendy's gaze flicked to the screen.

'It's James,' she said, picking it up.

Beth and Glen exchanged a glance.

'C'mon,' said Wendy. 'You said you wouldn't say anything. He's probably lost. Shall I meet you both there?' She answered the phone to James, standing and moving away from Beth and Glen and their knowing looks.

7

Eve and Jeff had decorated the Manor at the beginning of the month and so all of the lights were already in place. They twirled up the trunks of the trees that lined the driveway and in the grand hallway stood a tall, beautifully decorated Christmas tree, reaching up as the staircase curved around it. Just as Wendy remembered from her childhood. Her father's angel was perched on the top, looking as annoyed as ever at having a tree up her skirt. Wendy was just starting to get her head around the tables for the stalls when James finally found the Manor. She waved to him and gestured where he could park, out of the way but still in front of the house. He climbed out of the car, staring up at the building, mouth open. She approached, taking a deep breath.

'Sorry about the directions,' she said. 'Sometimes I forget it can be hard to find this place.'

'It's all right,' said James, still looking up at the house. 'This is where you grew up?'

'Yup.'

'It's huge!' James met her eyes. 'It's amazing.' He looked around her, out to the carefully maintained gardens that wrapped around the house. 'What's over there?'

She turned, following his gaze.

'Erm, the stalls for the fair?'

'No, the trees, past the hedge.'

'Oh, that's the orchard. We've got stalls going up along the drive, on the lawn, in the orchard and into the hall of the house. There'll be some food and drink stalls but we're also offering some of our own, my brother's girlfriend and my father's house-keeper are dealing with all that.'

'Housekeeper? You have a housekeeper?'

'No,' Wendy said slowly. 'My father's house-keeper. Janine. My brother kept her on after my father passed away. She's become part of the family. Jeff gave her the whole of December off as extra paid leave due to the wedding and honeymoon and then Christmas, but word travels fast in these parts and she got wind of what we were doing and has come to help. Thankfully. I don't really know where everything is.'

James whistled through his teeth.

'So, everything's under control? What do you want me to do?'

'My brother's checking on the set up in the orchard for the brass band we've got coming. Could you help him?'

'Sure.'

Wendy led the way across the front of the house to the orchard. She paused by Beth, setting up trestle tables.

'This is Beth, our saviour. My brother's girl-friend. She's the one who got us out of Sue's pickle.'

'As it were,' said Beth with a grin.

'And she makes a mean cake,' Wendy added with a smile. 'She's the creator of all the sweet stuff here today and on the day of the fair. Beth, this is James.' She subtly shot Beth a warning look.

Beth and James shook hands.

'Pleasure to meet you,' said Beth. 'I'd ask for a hand, seeing as how you look strong, but I'm guessing you're off to help the other strong man around here.'

'I'll come back and help you,' Wendy assured her, wandering towards the orchard. James said something to Beth that made her laugh and then followed.

In the small orchard, Glen was perched pre-cariously on a stepladder, reaching up to hook a cable to one of the P.A. system speakers.

'Glen?'

Glen wobbled as he looked over his shoulder. He gave up on the cable and turned on the stepladder.

'This is James. James, this is my big brother, Glen. James'll help you. Please don't fall off.' Wendy gave the stepladder a look. 'Be careful,' she told Glen, giving him the same meaningful look she'd given Beth.

Leaving the two men discussing cabling strategies, Wendy returned to helping Beth set up the tables.

'Well, he seems lovely,' said Beth in a low voice.

'Hmm.'

'And younger than I imagined. Although I don't know why. You said he was a junior.'

'He's older than I thought he would be,' Wendy told her. 'He had a career change in his late twenties.'

'Ah,' said Beth. 'Been there. Done that. Baked the celebration cake.'

Wendy grinned.

'Is it the age difference?' Beth asked. 'Is that the problem?'

Wendy's grin dropped. This again. She wasn't sure how much more of this she could take.

'No, Beth. There's no problem. Let's just get these tables up.'

The tables were ready along the front of the house when Glen appeared from the gardens, brushing his hands together.

'I just had a lovely chat with James,' said Glen, wandering over and slipping an arm around Beth's waist. Wendy froze.

'Oh god. What did you say? What did he say?' she blurted.

'Don't worry. I just asked him about his job. Did you know he used to be a tree surgeon?' Glen asked.

'You don't forget those skills. Could be very handy having someone like that in the family.' He looked over to the large, old trees that lined the driveway.

'Will you please stop talking like that,' Wendy said a little more harshly than she meant to.

Beth and Glen exchanged a glance and a smile.

'And stop doing that!' Wendy screeched.

Beth and Glen both jumped.

'What?' Glen asked, looking around them.

'That cute look you keep giving each other. That "we know things" look. I'm sick of it.' The words fell out of Wendy at a speed and volume she had no control over. 'We get it, you're in love and happy. And I'm happy that you found each other. And I'm happy that Jeff and Eve found each other. But you know what? Maybe some people just aren't meant to be all lovey-dovey. Maybe some people are meant to be on their own. And maybe some couples should stop rubbing it in everyone's faces. Okay? I'm sick of it. I'm great on my own. I'm doing great. I don't need anyone else and I don't need the two of you giving each other those stupid looks.'

Vision blurred, Wendy stormed away from Beth and Glen before either could reply. She headed into the house, head down, through the hall, straight through the kitchen, out the back door and into the back garden. She didn't slow. Over the lawn, strewn with the last of the season's dead leaves, to the very back where the ground became squelchy and the roses were dormant. In the corner was a swing wide

261

enough for two, tied by old rope to the branches of a large oak tree that had looked over the garden long before it had become a garden. Wendy's father had put the swing there for their mother and all three children had adopted it as their own. Now, Wendy gingerly sat on it, brushing angry tears from her eyes and instinctively giving herself a gentle push to put the swing in motion.

She didn't know how long she sat there, staring into nothing as the fresh memories of Beth and Glen and how she'd been feeling dwindled, pushed aside by older memories of sitting beside her mother on this swing. She could feel the warmth of her mother's arm around her, keeping her steady and safe. Tears dropped down her cheeks. There weren't words for how much she missed her mother so it always came as a gaping, agonising hole in her chest instead. She inhaled sharply, filling her lungs with the chill of December but that didn't take away the pain.

There was a rustle and the sound of footsteps in the mud. Wendy looked up and through her tears saw James making his way across the lawn. Hurriedly, she wiped her eyes dry on her sleeve, wondering how badly her make-up had smeared.

'Hey.' James approached cautiously, studying the swing. 'I can go if you want.'

Wendy sniffed.

'No. It's okay,' she murmured.

'You all right?' he asked, stepping closer.

Wendy nodded. She didn't trust herself to lie out loud.

'How old is that swing? Is it safe?'

Wendy looked up at the ropes.

'My dad made it before Glen was born. For my mum. It feels safe.' She shrugged and then shifted over. The swing lurched to the side until James pulled it level again and carefully sat beside her. They moved the swing back and forth in silence for a moment.

'Do you want to talk about it?' James finally asked, not looking at her.

'I don't know.'

'I know I'm not impartial or unbiased in this.'

Wendy glanced at him.

'Aren't you?'

James turned and met her gaze, his eyes softening.

'No. I like you,' he said bluntly.

A shot of pleasure erupted from Wendy's stomach and spread out to her toes and fingers.

'Oh,' she managed, looking back towards the garden.

'I think we all deserve to be happy,' James continued. 'Whether that's alone or with someone. I get it, you know. That you don't want to be with anyone. You have your kids to think about. And your career. You probably don't have time for a relationship.'

'No,' Wendy murmured. Her eyes ached.

'I mean, that's why things were weird between us this week. Right? We opened up, maybe started becoming friends. But you don't have time for that.'

Wendy turned to him.

'Is that what you think?'

James didn't reply but after a second, he gave her a sideways glance.

'That's not it at all,' Wendy told him. 'I would love for us to be friends.' She looked down at her muddy shoes. 'I could do with more friends. My husband seemed to get all of ours in the divorce.'

'Then why have things been weird?' asked James, his full attention on her.

Wendy sighed and looked up at her childhood home.

'I was unprofessional. I'm trying to make partner and do a good job, and I was supposed to be in charge and instead we got drunk.'

'And did the job,' James pointed out. 'And nothing happened. So what's the problem? No one knows. No one has to know. There's nothing to know.'

Wendy closed her eyes. He was right. She hadn't really done anything wrong, so why was she feeling like this?

'I had fun that night,' she said without opening her eyes.

James shifted his weight and the swing moved in answer.

'And you're not happy about that?'

Something clawed at Wendy. Wasn't that what Beth had pointed out to her? That she needed to have more fun? She used to have so much fun before she'd started acting like such a grown up.

'I think I'm not happy with how much I miss having fun,' she said in a voice barely audible. Still, James heard her.

'So you thought you'd hide away when on the other side of this massive house there's a Christmas fair being set up? I mean, I get that this swing is fun and all, but come on. Have you tasted Beth's mince pies? They're insanely good.'

Wendy laughed. The grin pulled at the tears dried on her cheeks and while it hurt, the twinge of pain was good.

'Come on,' said James. 'Let's get back to work. We've got a Christmas fair to run, you've got a promotion to get and I'm still counting down the days until January.'

'Okay,' agreed Wendy. 'But first we need to figure out how to get up from this swing without one of us falling off.'

8

There was still an hour to go before the metaphorical doors to the Christmas fair opened but everything was ready. Wendy wandered slowly down the grand staircase towards the hall, her gaze on her father's angel on top of the tree.

'Miss you, Dad,' she murmured as she passed it. The angel's wonky smile looked back at her. She paused on the step and sighed at the ache in her chest.

'Wow. You look amazing.'

Wendy jumped at the sound of James's voice. He was standing at the foot of the tree, a box of cupcakes in his arms, looking up the stairs at her. As their eyes met, he realised what he'd said and cleared his throat.

'I mean, that's a nice dress.'

Wendy smiled, holding the skirt of the dress out and doing a small swirl on the step.

'I used to have a dress like this when I was little,' she told him, walking down the stairs. 'It was my favourite. Glen reminded me of it. I forgot just how much I used to get into Christmas. So I did some shopping. I can't believe I managed to find a Santa dress like this. Time to get back to the real me, I think,' she added in a murmur.

'It's a good look on you,' said James, ripping his gaze back up to her eyes as she approached him.

'I thought you hated Christmas? Can't wait until January?' she teased.

'I do and I can't.' James looked down at the box of cupcakes in his arms. 'Although the food isn't bad.'

Wendy laughed.

'That's not even proper Christmas food. I make a mean roast potato.'

The corners of James's lips twitched up and for a moment, they smiled at each other, the lights of the tree twinkling around them. It was spoiled by James's phone ringing. Wendy took the cupcakes from him so he could answer. He made noises, nodded his head, sighed and ran a hand over his face. The longer the conversation went on, the bigger the ball of dread grew in Wendy's stomach.

'What?' she dared to ask as he hung up.

'So, err, turns out the coach company double booked us. They apologise profusely but they can't pick everyone up from London and drive them here.' James turned to look out of the porch and towards the Christmas fair, with stallholders setting up, ready and waiting for guests.

Wendy couldn't breathe. Her dress was too tight, her chest aching. She shoved the box of cupcakes back into James's arms as her hands began to tremble.

'Oh god,' she murmured. 'What're we going to do? Graham's in London. He's expecting a coach. All the partners are.' Her voice climbed higher as she spoke. There was a pause but her brain offered her nothing. Just icy, panicked silence.

'We could go get them,' James offered in a slow, thoughtful voice. Wendy turned to him, waiting for more. He glanced up at her. 'I don't suppose anyone in this town has a spare minibus or two?'

Wendy's brain kicked back into gear. Turning on her heel, she strode out of the house and into the fair.

'Beth?' she called. A stallholder pointed her in the right direction and she found Beth with her café manager and Eve's events assistant, Pete, setting up their bakery stall in the orchard. Out of breath, Wendy explained the problem. 'Do you know any-one who has a minibus?'

Beth, eyes wide, blinked and looked to Pete who pursed his lips in thought.

'My uncle lives in a village down the road,' he said. 'He runs a coach trip business and has a coach or two. I'm pretty sure he said he was taking this December off. He's getting ready to retire. I've no idea if he's around or not though. Pretty sure he said something about the Bahamas for Christmas.'

Beth and Wendy stared at him.

'How fortuitous,' said Beth.

'Can you call him?' asked Wendy.

Pete nodded and wandered off with his phone.

'I've called some local companies but no one's got anything available,' said James from behind them. Beth took the cupcakes from Wendy before she dropped them.

'Sit down,' Beth ordered, pointing to the chair behind the stall. Wendy did as she was told, her breathing coming fast, her head becoming light.

'All of this work for nothing,' she said under her breath.

'Rubbish,' Beth told her. 'We just need the right vehicles.'

'And people to drive them,' said Wendy. 'There's about a hundred people we need to get here from London.'

'They could get the train?' Glen offered, shrugging as the women turned on him. 'Nice dress, by the way,' he added. 'Just like the one from when we were kids. Where are your antlers?'

Wendy gave a weak smile. Now was really not the time.

'That's not a bad idea,' said James. 'At least some of them could get the train.'

'Think about it,' Wendy told him. 'If we tell them to get the train then we have to admit that the coaches have fallen through.'

'And you'll be proving that you can think on your

feet,' Glen pointed out.

'And it's more environmentally friendly than coaches,' Beth added. 'That has to score points, right?'

'Plus, I bet they'll see the train as an adventure,' James told her. 'It's worth a shot.'

'Mixed news.' Pete returned, sliding his phone back into his pocket. 'My uncle is abroad for Christmas but he does have one coach going spare. Says we can use it but we need someone with the right licence.'

'That's not a problem,' said James. 'I have a licence to drive a coach.'

In silence, they all turned to stare at him.

'What? Why?' Wendy shook her head. 'How many does the coach seat?' she asked Pete.

'About fifty.'

Wendy ran her fingers through her hair and groaned as her mind spun.

'Right.' She turned on James. 'We can pick up the partners and senior associates on the coach, tell everyone else to get the train?'

James quickly thought this through and then gave a singular nod, unlocking his phone.

'Tell me we're getting a refund on the coaches,' said Wendy.

'Definitely.' James flicked through his phone.

'Good. Can we get first class tickets for the people getting the train?'

James looked up and grinned.

'Great idea. Leave it with me.' He turned away and within seconds was holding the phone to his ear.

'Shall I give him a lift to my uncle's when he's done? To get the coach?' Pete offered.

'Please,' said Wendy. 'Thank you. Thank you so much.' She stopped herself from hugging him as she stood, her skirt swishing as she ran to catch up with James.

They might have arrived an hour later than expected, but eventually James drove the coach full of solicitors up the Manor's driveway. Wendy and Janine, the Manor's housekeeper, were ready to hand each person a glass of mulled wine or orange juice as they stepped off the coach. On the entrance to the fair, Beth and Glen handed out a mince pie each. Music was softly playing throughout the hall and grounds, lights were twinkling from the trees, along the stalls and around the porch of the house. Inside the house, the tall Christmas tree was lit up invitingly.

Kit was one of the first off the coach and she stared up at the house before giving Wendy a giddy squeal.

'This is amazing!' she hissed, taking a glass of mulled wine. 'Better than tinsel at my desk. I love that dress.'

'Thank you,' Wendy hissed back. 'Enjoy.'

Kit did something of a cackle and wandered off towards Beth and Glen, sipping her drink.

Graham stepped off the coach and took a mulled wine from Wendy, looking around and breathing in.

'Well,' he said. 'Impressive.' He gave her a smile before venturing forward with the others towards the scent of freshly baked mince pies.

The feeling of her shoulders easing down from her ears was immense. As the last person stepped off the coach, Wendy caught James's eye behind the wheel. He gave her a wink and she looked away hurriedly. Unable to wrench the grin from her face or control the fizzy warmth in her belly, Wendy made her way back to the house to restock on mulled wine, ready for the rest of the arrivals.

James managed to somehow reverse the coach down the driveway without hitting anything and picked up the remaining guests from the firm at the train station. They arrived soon after, giddy and chatty and already toasting Wendy before she could offer them the wine.

'I bought them champagne along with the first class tickets,' James told her as he climbed down from the coach. 'Hope that was okay.'

'Inspired,' Wendy told him, still smiling.

'Good. So, now we can relax?' James clapped his hands. 'Let's party.'

'You've done amazingly,' Wendy said. 'Go enjoy yourself. Relax.'

'What about you?'

'I'll relax when it's over.'

9

As the sun dipped below the horizon, turning the sky and few clouds a dusty pink, the twinkling fairy lights came into their own. Wendy turned on the outside lights properly, illuminating where the fairy lights couldn't reach, and helped the brass band to set up. They were friends of Eve's, playing at her Christmas fair and ghost tour every year, and had jumped at the chance of another gig. As they started playing, something quivered inside Wendy.

This was Christmas.

The brass band, the smell of mince pies, turkey sandwiches and mulled wine, the lights, the sound of happy chatter and laughter.

'I'd say this is a success,' said Graham, appearing behind her as she stepped back to survey what she and James had managed to create. Well, what Eve had managed to create from a distance, but she'd already told Wendy not to mention that.

'Thank you,' she said shortly. 'James deserves a lot of the credit.'

'Hmm. Quick thinking about how to get us all here. And this is a beautiful place. Your childhood home, I guess?'

'Yes.'

'Lovely. I'm impressed that you managed to put all of this together with such short notice.' Graham sipped at his drink. 'I'll be chatting with the partners about who will be promoted soon. We'll probably need some food for that.' Before Wendy could respond, Graham turned away and wandered off towards the food stalls.

Wendy exhaled slowly, her mouth dry. She needed a drink.

Purposefully going in the opposite direction to Graham, she found herself near the brass band and grabbed a glass of champagne from a table full of drinks and mince pies. She sipped at it, half closing her eyes, letting the music take over her thoughts.

'I reckon I can add successfully organising a Christmas fair to my CV.'

Wendy opened her eyes and turned to James, giving him a smile.

'Definitely,' she told him. 'And I'll put in a good word for you with Graham. You've done a brilliant job. Thank you so much for your help.'

'That's okay,' said James. 'It was nice to get to know you.'

One of Wendy's eyebrows twitched up in a playful question and James grinned.

'You know, professionally. As a senior associate.'

'It's good to network,' Wendy agreed and they both laughed, Wendy trying to keep the champagne bubbles from going up her nose.

'That's a good idea,' said James, looking down at her drink. He vanished for a moment and returned with his own glass of champagne.

'So, how come you have a coach driver's licence?' Wendy asked over the sound of the brass band as they started a new song. James pulled a face at the sudden change in tempo and gestured for Wendy to join him a little further away. There was an newly unoccupied bench that Wendy's father had placed in the orchard so he could enjoy the birds in the trees. They sat down and watched the fair around them.

'Would you believe that before I trained as a tree surgeon, I worked as a coach driver?'

'Really?' Wendy gave him a sceptical look.

'I lasted four weeks. I hated it.' James laughed. 'But I got the licence. It means I'm usually the designated driver for big group things.'

Wendy smiled.

'Well, I definitely appreciate it. This would have been a complete failure without you and your coach licence.'

James held up his glass.

'Anytime.'

Wendy clinked her drink against his.

'When will you hear about the promotion?' James asked as they sipped their drinks.

'Graham says they're deciding soon. So, soon? I guess. I don't know.' Wendy looked down at her shoes.

'What's wrong?'

Wendy sighed.

'I don't know. I like being home. Maybe it's the clash between home and work?' she ventured, glancing at James. The low fairy lights accented his features, making his eyes dance and sparkle, his hair shine, the stubble on his chin darker. A breeze moved through the orchard and Wendy automatically leaned closer to James's warmth as a chill snuck through her clothes. The scent of his aftershave, or whatever he was wearing, twisted her stomach pleasurably.

She leaned away.

'Maybe,' he murmured, watching her. 'Or maybe you don't want this promotion.'

Wendy looked at him.

'What? Of course I do. I've worked so hard for it.'

James smiled.

'Been there,' he said. 'Worked hard, got the promotion, found out I hated the job. Done that.'

'Going from tree surgeon, up trees all day, to managing tree surgeons and a business is very different from becoming a partner at a law firm,' Wendy told him. 'I don't think I'll have the same problem.'

'At a law firm in the centre of London that deals with all sorts of things,' James pointed out. 'That's why I wanted to work with them. I have no idea what area of law I want to work in. I thought this way, I could move around a bit. See what takes my fancy.'

'What are you getting at?'

James shrugged.

'I dunno. Just that this promotion shouldn't be the be-all and end-all. There are other options. Take it from the ex-tree surgeon turned solicitor who has a coach driving licence. Have you even tried anything other than being a solicitor?'

Wendy frowned.

'No. It's what I always wanted. Even in my teens, I did my work experience at the solicitors in town. Property conveyancing,' she added. 'It was okay.'

'And you stuck with it. What's so special about being a solicitor to you?'

Wendy met his gaze.

'I told you. To help people.'

'Good.' James leaned back on the bench, sliding an arm along the wooden back, reaching behind her. 'Just know there are other options.'

Wendy turned away, brow creased in thought.

'You know,' James added. 'Go with this whole you returning to being you thing.' He leaned forward, extracting his arm and downing the last of his champagne. 'Because I really do like you. This real you.' He stood and went to walk away. A flutter of panic went through Wendy.

'What are you doing for Christmas?' she blurted

out. Anything to keep him there, by her side. She wouldn't let herself dwell on why that was important.

James turned back.

'Christmas with my mum and stepdad, as usual. Then probably just watching films. My housemate's away so I'll have the place to myself.'

Wendy bit her lip, allowing herself to think before she said what her mouth was so eager to say.

'We always do a big Boxing Day here,' she told him, looking up to his eyes as he towered over her. 'Not just family. I cook and Beth brings pudding and things. And we sit by the fire and chat and eat. It's nice. You're very welcome to join us.'

James rocked back slightly.

'Oh. Well. That sounds... Thank you.'

'I know it sounds strange but, really, it won't be. My brothers will be there, and Beth and Eve. Janine, who you've already met. Glen's son. The two gardeners my father used to hire. Jeff kept them on too. And probably a couple of other people Jeff and Eve have invited.'

'And you can just invite me without asking them? To their house?'

Wendy grinned.

'Of course. They don't mind as long as I cook.'

'And you make the best roast potatoes,' James murmured. His soft voice slid beneath Wendy's coat and she shivered.

'Think about it,' she said in a voice equally low.

James searched her eyes, smiling, and opened his mouth to speak.

'There you are!' Beth appeared beside him. 'Time to announce how much money we've raised and bring this thing to a close. Come on, both of you.'

Somehow, without Eve's presence and know-how, they'd managed to successful rig up the P.A. system. Wendy and James settled themselves by the microphone. Wendy's heart gave a nervous flutter, her stomach gurgling in rebellion of the champagne. She cleared her throat as James gave her an encouraging smile. Pressing the button, she avoided James's eyes and found her voice.

'Hey there, colleagues,' she said. Her voice echoed around the fair and some of the chatter quietened to listen to her. 'The fair is drawing to a close and it's time to announce just how much money has been raised. First of all, a massive thank you to you. Thank you for coming. I know it's been different this year—'

'Better!' someone shouted.

Wendy grinned and struggled for a moment to remember what she was saying.

'So, thank you for helping to make this fair work. Thank you for coming all this way. And a big thank you to the stallholders, to the band, and to my little brother and his new wife who are currently away on their honeymoon for letting us use their beautiful home. Over now to James, who helped put this fair together and is your designated driver for the evening.'

A cheer went up through the fair. Wendy passed the microphone to James.

'Hey everyone,' said James, a tremble of nerves in his voice. 'It's my pleasure to tell you that we have raised – and this money will be split between the three charities chosen by the firm for this year –' He paused for dramatic effect. 'One thousand, six hundred and fifty-three pounds.' He looked up at Wendy with wide eyes as he read the number from the paper Beth handed him. A loud murmur and some applause sounded through the fair. Grinning, James passed the microphone back to Wendy.

'That's... That's incredible. Thank you all so much,' she said, her voice ringing out. She couldn't be sure but wasn't that more than last year? 'Please enjoy the rest of your evening. We'll be shutting the gates in one hour so get those last minute presents bought, grab the last of the wine and food, and safe journey home. Merry Christmas. See you all in the New Year.'

A cheer went up around the fair and the volume of voices rose as some people scrambled for the drinks tables while others rushed back to buy that thing they'd been putting off.

Beth placed her hand on Wendy's shoulder and squeezed.

'Congratulations,' she murmured, bending to give her a quick hug.

'I'd best get the coach ready to go,' said James.

'But, you were drinking champagne,' Wendy realised, heart pounding in new panic. James waved her away.

'One small glass. It's the only alcohol I've had today. I'm fine. Trust me.'

Wendy smiled, staring into his dark chocolate eyes. She did trust him. How could she not after what they'd managed to create together?

'Wendy.' Graham appeared as James made his exit. Tapping her elbow, Graham gestured for her to follow him. They stopped in a corner, out of the way, and Graham grinned.

'You've raised more money than any of our fairs in the last four years. Congratulations.'

'Wow. Thank you.' Wendy's mouth had gone dry. He hadn't just pulled her over here to tell her what a good job she'd done.

'I've had my meeting with the partners and...' He paused for a beat. 'I'm delighted to offer you the promotion to partner. So, a double congratulations.' Graham beamed. 'You more than deserve it.'

Wendy had been waiting all of her adult life, and some of her childhood, to hear those words. She'd rehearsed this moment so many times, practising humility and enthusiasm. Would she punch the air? Would she cry? Would her chest burst from happiness? She'd been so eager to find out just how she would react to this moment.

The reality was something she had never expected. Her heart didn't pound, her chest didn't want to burst, she didn't feel like punching the air, in fact she hardly moved. She had to remind herself to smile before realising that wasn't enough. She grinned. A grin was more appropriate when accepting the promotion she'd been waiting so long for.

'That's incredible,' she told Graham. 'Thank you so much.'

If any of her struggles showed, he didn't seem to notice. Instead, he grabbed her hand and shook it.

'No, thank you. You saved all our bacon with this fair. You always seem to save our bacon, come to think of it. You're a fantastic solicitor, Wendy. I'll get HR on the paperwork first thing in the New Year but until then, rest assured that you're going into next year as partner. Now, go celebrate. Merry Christmas.'

'Thanks. Merry Christmas, Graham.'

Wendy's hand was still warm from his handshake as Graham wandered off to find one last glass of mulled wine before getting on the coach. She looked down at her hand and then up at the fair around her. Slipping out of the hall and onto the Manor's driveway, she bent her head back to stare up at the stars overhead, hugging herself against the cold.

She hadn't rehearsed for this reaction.

10

Wendy was on her feet half way through the knock on the door.

'I'll get it!' she called to whoever was listening. Beth giggled as Wendy walked past until Glen nudged her quiet.

'Do I need to do anything in the kitchen?' Jeff shouted after her.

'Yeah, stay out of it,' Wendy called back. She stopped in the chill of the hall, away from the roaring fire, and straightened her dress, checking her hair and pulling off the soft antlers Glen had bought her. Then, she opened the front door.

James looked up with wide eyes which softened when he saw her. He smiled, and while his eyes danced nervously, his smile was warm.

'Hey,' he murmured. 'Merry Christmas.' He brandished a bottle of wine.

'Hey. Welcome. Come in. I'm so glad you could come.' Wendy stood aside to let him in. 'Here, find a hook for your coat.'

James handed her the wine.

'Thank you,' she said. 'You really didn't need to bring anything.'

'Of course I did,' said James. 'But what do you bring the family with a professional baker, a couple who own a massive manor house and the person who makes the best roast potatoes? I hope it's okay.'

'It's more than okay,' said Wendy before wondering what on earth that meant and why she couldn't just say something normal. She paused before leading James into the living room. He stopped behind her.

'Everything all right?'

She nodded, taking a deep breath. Turning to face him, she smiled.

'I don't want this to be weird,' she told him. 'I'm really glad you're here,' she added in a quieter voice. Christmas had been difficult without the children, although she'd spoken to them on the day. Jeff, Eve, Beth and Glen had kept her busy but the darkness and chill of the evening and night had become almost painful. Boxing Day was proving better but there had still been something missing. An Emma and Oliver shaped hole. James didn't fill that, as such, but his presence had immediately brought a calmness to the part of her that missed them so much. He wasn't a distraction. This was something else.

James's eyes softened and something inside

Wendy softened with them.

'You know what?' he asked gently.

'What?'

'This was the first Christmas in a long time where everything felt all right. I wasn't counting down to January.'

'Really?'

'Yeah. I was counting down to Boxing Day instead.'

Wendy grinned and for a moment, she was certain that James leaned towards her. A loud peel of laughter broke into her thoughts and they moved away from one another.

'Are you ready?' Wendy asked.

James shrugged his shoulders, adjusting his shirt.

'Ready.'

Wendy led James into the living room, the warmth of the fire hitting them both in just the right way. Faces turned to them, all rosy cheeks and happy smiles.

'Everyone,' Wendy declared. 'This is James. Please be nice. James, this is everyone. Harry and Dave, my father's gardeners. You know Janine. And this is Rob, Glen's son.'

'Good to see you again,' said Glen, standing and slapping James on the back. 'Drink?'

'Please.' James glanced at Wendy. He followed Glen into the kitchen and Wendy followed James.

'Wine? Red? White? Tea? Coffee? Sherry?'

James blinked.

'Erm. What's everyone else drinking?'

Glen blew out his cheeks.

'Beth's on the tea, if that helps?' he offered. 'Beer?'

James chuckled.

'Beer. Thanks.'

Wendy stared at the occupants of the kitchen.

'James, this is my little brother Jeff who owns the house now and who I told not to go into the kitchen. Jeff, this is James.'

'Great to finally meet you.' Jeff and James shook hands. 'And I just came in for one of Beth's cookies.' Jeff held up his hands in surrender. 'She made me.' He pointed at Eve who guiltily waved a cookie at Wendy.

'We're eating soon,' said Wendy.

'I know. That made it more exciting,' said Eve. 'Jeff even provided some theme music while I checked for booby traps.'

There was a silence in the kitchen until Jeff and James both burst out laughing. Wendy rolled her eyes, smiling, before shooing them both out of the way of the oven.

'James, my new sister-in-law Eve.'

'Congratulations on getting married,' James told Jeff and Eve. 'And thanks for letting us use your house for the fair. This place is amazing.'

Jeff and Eve looked lovingly at one another.

'Isn't it,' Eve breathed.

Glen handed James a beer, opening one for himself.

'So, how was your Christmas? Wendy said you don't like Christmas. Has she changed your mind on it yet?' he asked.

James watched Wendy.

'Nearly,' he murmured.

'Taste her roast potatoes and then give her another year. You'll be decorating your desk with tinsel in no time.'

'Yeah, I imagine you'll be changing the rules on Christmas decorations in the office now you're partner, huh?' said James, sipping his beer. He stopped when no one responded. Wendy shuffled her feet, wondering how to word her next sentence. It turned out she needn't have worried, Glen did it for her.

'She didn't tell you? You guys haven't been talking since the fair? Wendy, why didn't you tell him you turned the job offer down?'

'What?' James spluttered.

Slowly, Wendy turned to face him.

'Why didn't you tell me?' James asked, which was a reasonable question seeing as they had been messaging one another since the fair. 'Why did you say no?'

'Time to go!' Eve declared, grabbing another cookie while she thought Wendy was distracted. Jeff hummed softly as Eve led him out of the kitchen. Glen stayed put until Wendy gave him a look.

'Oh. Yeah, best, erm, go see what Beth's up to. Might go find some mistletoe.' He elbowed James playfully and then quickly left.

Alone in the kitchen, James turned his focus on Wendy.

'I'm sorry I didn't mention it. I didn't know how,' she explained. 'I guess I was a bit embarrassed.'

'Embarrassed? Why?'

'I went on and on about this promotion. I've been going on and on about it all year. Well, all my life, it feels. And then I finally get it, and heaven knows I worked for it, and then I reject it. Sometimes, when I put it that way, it feels like I'm going a bit mad.' She glanced up at him, wondering how he would react.

He watched her, a smile curling up the corners of his lips. He placed his beer on the worktop and stepped closer.

'I know the feeling,' he said eventually, his voice low. 'You're not going mad.'

Her stomach flipped, heart pounding, unable to take her eyes from his.

'You're just becoming more you,' he continued. 'Do you know what you're going to do instead?'

Wendy nodded.

'I was thinking of starting my own firm. It was something Beth said to me. And something you said at the fair, about everything being spread out, helping so many different people in so many different ways. When I was young, I wanted to help the people who couldn't afford the big, shiny London solicitors. So that's what I'm going to do.'

'Some would argue that isn't the best way of making money,' said James.

'Well, maybe I didn't become a solicitor for the money after all.'

They stared at one another for a long time. James stepped closer just as a nagging feeling dawned on Wendy.

'Oh, the potatoes.'

She turned from him and opened the oven. Steam erupted, pushing James away, and Wendy pulled out the tray of roast potatoes and vegetables, giving it a shake and placing it on the hob.

'Wow.' James peered over her shoulder. 'They look good.'

'Told you,' she murmured, turning her head to find him irresistibly close. She caught his eyes and for a moment, she wondered if he would kiss her. Or if she should lean forward and kiss him.

The smoke alarm on the ceiling by the back door began beeping, making both of them jump.

'Damn.' Wendy moved to close the oven as James pounced on the back door to open it. Wendy pointed to the button she didn't have a hope in reaching to turn the alarm off and James pulled over a chair to stand on in order to press it.

'Everything okay?' Jeff appeared at the door. 'You never set the smoke alarm off.'

'Sorry. Sorry, I opened the oven door and forgot to open the back door and... I think we're nearly ready. Go check the table,' said Wendy, surveying the food.

Jeff nodded and left them alone again.

'Have you told Graham yet?' James asked, waving a tea towel at the smoke alarm to stop it from going off again. 'About your new firm dream?'

Wendy nodded, pouring herself a glass of wine.

'I've already handed my notice in.'

'Wow. It's really happening.'

'Yeah.' Wendy sipped her drink.

'Nervous?'

Wendy gave that some thought.

'No, actually.' She grinned at James. 'I mean, a little bit but more excited, I think.'

'That means it's the right thing,' James told her, slowly moving closer. 'How long is your notice?'

'Three months. Enough to get the foundations of the new business up and running.'

'So, in three months we won't be working together anymore.'

Wendy looked up into those dark eyes of his.

'No. We won't.'

Did that mean what she thought it meant? Would working together have stopped them?

'I really do like you, Wendy.'

Wendy, mouth dry and heart pounding, smiled.

'I really like you too.'

James stepped up to her and leaned down. She

went up on tiptoe without thinking until their lips met. The kiss was slow, although it probably only lasted seconds. His lips were warm and tangy with the taste of beer. He inhaled as they kissed, breathing her in. She rocked back as they parted, checking the door behind James. No one was there, no one was watching. No one was watching her other than James. His full attention was on her, his eyes soft.

'And there's not even any mistletoe,' she murmured.

James clicked his fingers.

'Knew I'd forgotten something.'

They gazed into one another's eyes for a delicious moment, both smiling until Wendy's thoughts offered her something.

'It's strange,' she said, the back of her mind piecing things together despite her urgent need to kiss James again before anyone walked in. 'Two years ago, my father passed away and weeks later, on the day before Christmas Eve, Jeff and Eve got together. Now they're married. Beth and Glen met that Boxing Day and, you know, I think that's when I realised my marriage was over. Last year, Beth and Glen finally got together on Boxing Day and a month later, I was getting divorced. And now, here we are, Boxing Day and I'm kissing a gorgeous, intelligent man in my father's kitchen.'

James smiled, sliding an arm around her waist. She allowed him to pull her closer.

'You think it's all connected?' he asked.

'Jeff said something weird happened when he and Eve got together. Pictures of Jeff falling off the walls in front of Eve. Like Dad was still here, pushing them together. And Beth and Glen wouldn't have met if they hadn't gotten together.'

'We would still have met. We might even still be kissing right now,' James told her, his thumb stroking her side.

Wendy shook her head.

'I would still be married,' she said quietly, the realisation hitting her like a brick. She put her hand on James, mostly for support. 'Dad knew I was unhappy. He knew. He left me that money for the divorce.' She looked up at the ceiling.

'You think he's still here? Watching over you?' James asked, wrapping his other arm around her in a hug.

'Maybe. Maybe he's making sure we're all happy.' Wendy looked into James's eyes.

'Are you happy?' he asked.

Wendy smiled.

'Do you think this is the magical story of how we got together?' she asked quietly, hoping that he wouldn't hear if he didn't have the answer she wanted.

'Well, I was hoping that Graham introducing us to organise the Christmas fair would be the magical story of how we got together. But I quite like this version too.'

Wendy stared up at him, her eyes widening.

'When Graham introduced us?' she asked.

James nodded.

'Are you kidding? Boss comes over with this beautiful woman, lost in her own thoughts, and tells me to do whatever I can to help her. He barely had to ask.'

Wendy's cheeks burned and she looked away, staring into his chest. He leaned down to catch her eye and pull her gaze back up.

'Wendy, you made me like Christmas. That's big. Even my mum and stepdad noticed yesterday, they kept asking me what had changed. And it's you. You've changed something in me. In only a week, you managed to make me smile throughout Christmas.'

Wendy couldn't stop the grin.

'And you haven't even tasted my roast potatoes yet.'

James laughed and the sound sent a thrill through her.

'Imagine what you'll be doing to me by the summer,' he murmured, leaning down.

'Good things, I hope,' she said, wrapping her arms around his neck.

James sobered for a moment.

'I promise,' he said, their lips almost touching. 'We will always celebrate Christmas however you want. I want you to always be you.'

Wendy pushed forward and kissed him, softly at

first, becoming harder as her hands went into his hair. He lifted her, pulling her closer and Wendy smiled into the kiss.

'Really happy you're together and don't want to interrupt, but can we eat yet?' came Beth's voice from the other side of the kitchen door.

James let go of Wendy but she hung on. The kiss broke and they laughed softly.

'Coming,' Wendy called around James, giving him one last kiss before letting him go and turning back to the oven. 'We'll continue this after we've eaten.'

'And every time we go into a kitchen, and whenever the kids are distracted by the TV or something,' James murmured in her ear, kissing her cheek before reaching for the plates.

Wendy grinned as she began to dish up, something inside her melting at the mention of her children. The ache in her chest from missing them joined with a warmth in her gut that was almost that feeling of coming home for Christmas. For the first time in longer than she could remember, she truly relaxed as James bustled beside her and the sounds of her family chatting and laughing filtered through from the next room.

They carried the first platters of food through, leaving the kitchen behind them. Through the kitchen window, out in the darkness of the Boxing Day evening, around the trees and the swing made for two, snowflakes slowly began to fall.

This is the last book in this mini novella trilogy. If you enjoyed these stories, please consider leaving a rating or review to help other readers find the Hargreaves family.

.

LOOKING FOR YOUR NEXT ROMANCE?

Try **Digging The Director**,

A Scottish Christmas Dream

and

Let's Skip This Christmas

by Jennifer Nice.

Find your next read and
sign up to the mailing list at
www.writeintothewoods.com/romance

ACKNOWLEDGEMENTS

Thank you to Jeff and Eve Hargreaves.

I had so much fun writing about you in the horribleness that was 2020. You brought light and joy to a dark year.

And look at what you started!

Also, a massive thank you to the non-fictional people in my life.

A sweet thank you to Vicky of Tallulah's Bakery for being not just a friend but the Queen of Sugar Biscuits.

My husband for understanding when I had to disappear upstairs to write after watching Bake Off. My dad for smiling and nodding while I discuss Christmas romance with my mum. And my mum, for sharing with me her passion for romance stories and encouraging me down this route.

Printed in Dunstable, United Kingdom